Grimm

Books by Mike Nicholson

Catscape
Grimm

For younger readers

Museum Mystery Squad
... and the Case of the Moving Mammoth
... and the Case of the Hidden Hieroglyphics
... and the Case of the Curious Coins
... and the Case of the Roman Riddle
... and the Case of the Vanishing Viking

For wee ones

Thistle Games
Thistle Street
Thistle Sands

Grimm

Mike
Nicholson

Kelpies is an imprint of Floris Books

This edition published in 2008 by Floris Books

Second printing 2019

www.florisbooks.co.uk

Also available as an eBook

British Library CIP Data available

ISBN 978-086315-668-7

To my Mum and Dad who kept Grimm's fires burning by always asking for the next chapter.

To Joy, Joseph and a double mention for Theo who missed out last time; the best distractions I have from writing.

Contents

Grimm Grimm as grim as can be
You sit on the hill that has no tree

Grimm Grimm on rocks so high
Your guests go mad and then they die

Grimm Grimm throughout the years
You've brought sadness, death and tears

Grimm Grimm where no one goes
Except the rats and bats and crows

Grimm Grimm go if you dare
But you might not come back from there

Local Skipping Song

Prologue

In the gathering gloom, the crows slowly circled the turrets and spires. Perched precariously on a pinnacle of rock, the hotel looked as though the next breath of wind might topple it down the hillside. A pin-prick of light appeared and then disappeared as a door opened and closed again. A shadowy figure limped to the dilapidated station that housed the machinery. Moments later with a growl and a grind, a cable car emerged and creaked out on sagging hawsers into the night-time sky. To the sound of small rusty wheels turning, it left the huge flat rock ledge before swinging above the flatter grassy slopes of Scrab Hill, towards the sleeping town of Aberfintry.

At the bottom, a squat stocky figure met the cable car as it clattered into the ground level station then, carrying something, the person headed into the quiet streets of the town, seeking out the letterbox of an ordinary house. In his hand he clutched an envelope sealed with blood-red wax and stamped with the mark of a snarling wolf's head.

1. The wax-sealed envelope

Rory looked in the mirror and wondered if he would ever get the chance to do so again. The letter was lying discarded on his bed. Its contents hadn't changed, much as he had willed them to. He tried to weigh up their significance. Surprising? Yes. Worrying? Absolutely. Dangerous? Almost certainly. Rory groaned and stared at his pale, tense reflection. There was not the hint of a smile. His brown eyes looked tired, and his short dark hair spiked up because he had run his hands through it a dozen times, in as many anxious minutes. It was a far cry from the beaming Rory McKenna clutching the shiny plaque who looked down at him from the framed photo above his bed.

"What are you grinning at?" Rory said bitterly to the picture of himself. "It's all your fault anyway."

He trudged to the window, passing the neatly stacked tower of Zizz Cola cans in the corner of his room. Topped up whenever he wanted, it sat reminding Rory of his "achievement," yet the thought of opening and drinking one now made him feel sick. Looking out into a blustery evening sky, Rory could see the brooding silhouette of Hotel Grimm high up on Scrab Hill. He swallowed hard and shuddered. Normally, Rory's approach to life would be to ignore the difficult things and just hope that they would drift away, but this was different … very different. He closed his eyes and groaned. The letter lay curled up, a seemingly innocent sheet of paper, the contents of which had definitely ruined his day …

2. Four months earlier

"Ladies and Gentlemen, will you please put your hands together and give your warmest welcome to the quite remarkable ... Rory McKenna."

The room burst into applause from the candle-lit tables. The men in dinner jackets and the stunningly-dressed women craned their heads to see Rory's short figure weave his way between the chairs. Rory began to feel very hot under his collar, which was unsurprising since he rarely wore a shirt and tie. Camera flashes exploded around him and he was aware of a sea of smiling faces, none of whom he knew, but all applauding him as he made his way to the stage.

"It's my great pleasure to present this award to Rory," boomed the loud American voice. "Rory's impact on our business has been nothing short of phenomenal. At the age of just eleven, he has succeeded in doing for Zizz Cola what most marketing professionals can only dream about, and his contribution has led to the most remarkable business story of the year. This recognition at tonight's International Marketing Awards Ceremony is a fitting thank you to this young man."

A plaque was thrust into Rory's hands and he was gently pushed to the front of the stage. Looking out, he could hardly make out the back of the vast room.

"You lucky wee rascal!" The thought of his

Grandad drifted into Rory's head and made him smile as he gazed out.

Despite himself, Rory was really quite enjoying all of this. However, as he stood soaking it in, another more niggling voice flitted into his mind. *Funny isn't it ... it was really nothing to do with you.*

A photographer shouted for him to turn and hold the plaque aloft, and Rory pushed this more troubling thought to the furthest corner of his mind and enjoyed the moment.

3. One year ago

Sitting in the blazing sun outside Aberfintry's Art Gallery Café, Rory put the ice-cold glass of Zizz Cola to his face and thought he could hear his skin sizzle. It was easily the hottest day of the summer so far. On the way there he'd seen hairy dogs desperate for a haircut, and people struggling to eat ice creams as they melted quicker than they could be eaten. Now, as the sun bounced off the metal tables at the café, Rory relaxed with his cold drink and watched as people all around did their best to get comfortable in the heat. On a beautiful day like today, facing away from Scrab Hill, you could almost forget about the hotel and its catalogue of disastrous events; not to mention the extraordinary shadow it had cast over the town for years.

The only significant movement was from a little girl skipping past, off to play amongst the sculptures positioned throughout the gallery's walled garden. Seemingly refreshed after her cold drink, she was singing as she went.

"It's fi-zzy, it's light, Zizz has got it right … It's fi-zzy, it's light, Zizz has got it right … It's fi-zzy, it's light, Zizz has got it right."

Rory took a long deep drink of Zizz, smacked his lips noisily and sighed out loud as he slumped back in his chair, letting the sun soak in. He was going to be in for a bit of a wait. He was with his Mum, who was off speaking to the Gallery Manager about an idea for another of her wacky exhibitions. Morag McKenna — or "Momo" as she had restyled herself since her artistic career had taken off — waved her arms and "oohed" and "aahed" just a little more than Rory could cope with these days. Sitting back in peace and quiet, and shutting his eyes to it all, was a much better option.

"Another satisfied customer!" drawled a voice with an American accent.

It took Rory a moment to realize that the comment had been addressed to him. He opened his eyes and squinted. The sun was blocked by a very large man in a voluminous suit putting his tray down at the adjacent table.

"Sorry, that was rude of me, but I couldn't help but notice how much you were enjoying your drink."

"Oh …?" said Rory, not really sure what else to say.

"Can I be even ruder and ask why you chose to drink Zizz Cola today?" said the man sitting down. He shifted a giant plate of sandwiches and a glass of water from his tray and looked at Rory. Momentarily flummoxed at being asked this question by a complete stranger, Rory could only say, "Well I … it's a hot day … I needed a cold drink."

"But why Zizz? You could just have had a glass of water like me. Or a nice refreshing fruit juice. Or even milk … I often think we can forget how good milk tastes, don't you?" said the man looking at Rory and taking an enormous bite from a sandwich.

"Umm ... yeah, but I felt like a can of Zizz today," Rory said, not quite sure what the man was angling after.

"You're going to think me a bit persistent but I really do wanna know why," persisted the stranger.

"I like the taste," said Rory, now a little irritated that his relaxing time in the sun had turned into a full-blown interrogation.

"Okay ... so what do you like about the taste?"

"I dunno ... it's just ... Er ... well, I just like the taste," said Rory. This answer did not satisfy the man, who put down his sandwich and leaned forward with a curious intensity.

"Mmm ... I appreciate that, but I'm after a USP here," said the man.

Rory looked blank.

"USP? ... Unique Selling Point ... What makes Zizz stand out for you?" said the man, wiping the side of his mouth with a napkin. "Let's try it this way. If you were describing that glass of Zizz Cola to a friend of yours to encourage them to try it, what would you say?"

Rory thought for a moment and then the girl's song from a few moments before suddenly popped into his head.

"It's fizzy, it's light, Zizz has got it right," said Rory, hoping that this would satisfy the man.

Easing himself back in his seat the man appeared distracted for a moment. He tilted his head to one side as if he was straining to hear something. For the first time he seemed unable to respond.

"Huh, well I'll be ..." was all that he managed.

Then looking into the distance he repeated what Rory had said, in a slow, quiet voice. "It's fizzy, it's light, Zizz has got it right … it's fizzy, it's light, Zizz has got it right! You're right, you know. That's exactly right."

The man pushed his plate to one side as if he had lost his appetite. He reached into his inside jacket pocket. "I'm gonna give you my card," he said.

"A card?" Rory felt lost once again.

"My business card," said the man who was now opening a slender and shiny metal case.

"Er … why?" asked Rory.

"I may need to contact you that's all, and I will definitely need to speak to your parents." Reaching over, the man handed Rory a stiff polished card with a razor sharp edge. In embossed lettering it read "HARVEY FINKLEMAN. CHIEF EXECUTIVE OFFICER, ZIZZ COLA." It gave contact details in Seattle, USA.

For a brief moment, Rory began to think that maybe he should let this Mr Finkleman know that the line he had just come out with had been someone else's. He couldn't see the girl who had skipped past, and just at that moment Rory's Mum returned to the table.

"Is this your boy, ma'am?" said Finkleman to Mrs McKenna.

"Yes, he's mine," said Mrs McKenna, flicking a wisp of red hair from her face. "Er … is there some kind of problem?"

"Not at all, ma'am … not at all. In fact your son has been extremely insightful … *extremely* insightful."

"Insightful?" said Mrs McKenna, fluttering her

enormous eyelashes and throwing a wide-eyed look in Rory's direction. "I suppose it runs in the family." Rory rolled his eyes.

"Well, buddy," said Finkleman addressing Rory with a look of understanding, "I don't really mind wherever it's come from as long as it's there. Now if you could give me an email address or number, I'll keep you posted with developments." He handed over a silver pen and reversed one of his cards for Rory to write on.

"I was about to write a few postcards to keep some family members happy, but if you'll excuse me, I think it may be time to cut this trip short as I have some calls to make. I'm going to wake them up Stateside but I think it's going to be worth it."

Finkleman passed a few polite words about the weather with Mrs McKenna as Rory scribbled down some contact details. Rory's mum managed to steer the subject to her recent meeting with the Gallery Manager and she began to enthuse about her idea for an exhibition on the theme of 'maroon.'"

"It's a colour that people just think is a kind of red. But it has its own inner beauty. It's been lost over time … 'marooned' you could say. We need to find it again," she said with wild intense eyes, rattling bangles as her arms waved and entangling her dangly earrings in her hair.

After a few polite grunts, the bulky American managed to use his urgent need to make an international phone call as an excuse to leave the table. He said his goodbyes, clutching a bundle of unwritten postcards and headed away, leaving a largely untouched lunch, a bewildered boy and a woman trying to get her jewellery under control.

Two days were just long enough for Rory to have almost forgotten about the encounter at the café, but then an e-mail from Harvey Finkleman popped into the inbox as Rory sat at the computer.

"Er, Dad ...?"

Rory's father was in his favourite armchair to one side of the fireplace, but as usual he was half-hidden. His legs were visible, as were his hands. The rest of him was behind the paper. Rory sometimes felt he was forgetting what his dad looked like given the amount of time he spent in this position. Ken McKenna's job as a driving instructor was another factor that meant Rory rarely saw him. People seemed to want to learn to drive just after school or work or at some point in the evening. Rory's brief exchanges with his dad took place as they passed on the garden path or bumped into each other at the bottom of the stairs near bedtime.

"Dad...?" tried Rory again.

"Mmmmm?" came the usual collection of 'm"s from behind the paper.

"Do we know anyone with a legal background?" asked Rory.

"Malky Mackay," said Mr McKenna in his typically distracted fashion as he turned another page.

"I don't mean a policeman," said Rory. "I mean a lawyer."

The newspaper pages rustled again. “Lachlan Stagg,” said his Dad. “Law was definitely one of his record-breaking list of qualifications.”

“Preferably one who is still alive,” mumbled Rory, looking over the email for a second time.

> It was a real pleasure to meet you in your cute little town the other day. Back in Seattle, I called an emergency meeting of my marketing department. All are agreed that your slogan exactly captures how we want to promote Zizz Cola in our new global campaign.
>
> One further development is that we would also like to film you saying the catch-phrase for the TV adverts we will be making soon.
>
> Naturally some reimbursement will be due to you for the intellectual property of the slogan and for your appearance in any filming.
>
> I’ll get my legal team to draw up a contract and will send you a draft copy for your lawyer to look over.

4. The marketing genius

With the arrival of that e-mail, Rory McKenna's rather odd double life began. He remained an ordinary schoolboy with a football to kick about at break-time, classes to trudge between and homework to puzzle over at the kitchen table. But at the same time his face and voice were about to go global.

It didn't take long for the filming of adverts to take place. Treated like a filmstar for a week, Rory enjoyed every minute lounging in his seat with his name on the back of it. He decided that he could get quite used to the life; sitting around, watching all the action as harassed people hurried past, barking into mobile phones, while amazing camera equipment was wheeled backwards and forwards. Every now and then someone would come and check he was okay and offer him something to eat or drink. Rory only wished this new lifestyle could be permanent. It certainly beat turning up on a Tuesday morning for double maths followed by cross-country running in the rain. At that stage, Rory could not have known that he would have opted for running extra laps wearing just a pair of pink pants to avoid what was going to happen next.

A period of relative calm followed for a month or two, but then Rory was half-watching TV after school one day when he suddenly appeared on the screen in front of himself, clutching a can of Zizz. It was a tingling, exciting but slightly scary moment and sure enough life changed almost immediately.

"It's fizzy, it's light, Zizz has got it right." The slogan was beginning to haunt him as half the school decided it was hilarious to mimic his line from the advert. It was shouted at him in the corridors by guffawing pupils he didn't even know, while others like the Goodman twins, Gracie and Gordon, delighted in making up alternatives: "He's got an ugly face, Ro-ry's a waste of space." It seemed to Rory that he had become their new target. The Goodmans were literally double the trouble of any normal school bully. They worked as a double act, which got them twice the laughs that any one person would.

"What's McKenna's USP?" Gracie would shout.

"Ugly Stupid and Pathetic!" Gordon would retort.

Meanwhile, even without the Goodmans' efforts, the less confident pupils at the school whispered, "That's him there," as Rory tried to have a quiet lunch in the dinner hall. He began to spend more time alone as some of his own friends drifted away not wanting to be part of the attention that he now attracted.

Even outside school, Rory attracted comments from passers by. PC Malky Mackay stopped his bike one day and asked him with a deadpan expression if he felt that he needed police protection. "I'll give it to you in return for an autograph," the lanky policeman had shouted after him.

Rory couldn't quite believe that his desire to avoid fuss by omitting to say that the slogan was someone else's, was now causing such complications in his life.

The real change for Rory came when Zizz announced their sales figures. Previously a relatively small player in the soft drinks world, Zizz had suddenly shot to the top of the charts like bubbles to the top of an opened bottle. They gave full credit for this sharp rise in sales to their new advertising campaign and to "the Zizz Boy," as Rory was now being called. As time went on, Rory began to realize that *he* had become the drink's unique selling point. He was sure that the slogan on its own would only have created half of the success, but with him in tow, there was an added human interest story.

Soon, the Business Pages section of almost every broadsheet paper covered the fact that Zizz's triumph as the top-selling drink had arisen out of a chance conversation between its Chief Executive Officer and an eleven-year-old boy. After that, the Sunday supplements picked up on the story and Mr McKenna had even more excuse to spend his time behind newspapers. Interest soon spread further afield as *Blue Peter* asked Rory to launch a competition to come up with a new slogan for the programme. Gracie and Gordon Goodman sparked off a new craze after that, of mimicking the *Blue Peter* music any time Rory passed by. Sometimes it was like the whole stairwell of the school was ringing with it as everyone joined in, much to the delight of the twins, whose sniping nasty laughs you could not tell apart.

Despite all of the national newspaper interest, Aberfintry's local paper *The Chronicle,* was very slow off the mark, eventually running an article entitled "Fizz Ahoy! Our Local Zizz Boy!" Rory had never met anyone from the paper although he knew that it was the Goodman twins' father, Derek, who wrote and edited the weekly publication. The article about him seemed to have been pieced together using information from everything else that had been published so far, along with quotes from people in the town who claimed to know Rory well, but who he had no recollection of meeting. *The Chronicle* also highlighted the fact that as the youngest ever recipient of an international marketing award, Rory could be following in the footsteps of Aberfintry's much-loved and much-missed Lachlan Stagg, who had been famous for amassing his own horde of wildly different world records.

After the publicity came the offers. All sorts of opportunities to endorse other products began to arrive as Rory was offered money to help in advertising everything from fishfingers to toilet paper. Even some of the rival drinks companies wanted to film him with their can in his hand saying, "Do you know what? I've changed my mind. This one's better."

Rory knew that things had gone completely mad when a suggestion came in to turn the slogan into a ringtone and a draft contract appeared offering the chance to record a song called "Merry Zizzmas," to try to get a Christmas number 1.

"I mean, have you ever heard me sing?" said Rory despairingly, as he shuffled through another selection of envelopes containing random offers of work at the end of a normal school day.

"Mmmmm," said his Dad lowering the paper for a rare moment. "I might draft a rival contract offering you the chance *not* to make a record."

Also arriving thick and fast were requests for Rory's expertise. Lots of companies now saw Rory as the marketing wizard who had cracked the challenge for Zizz and they wanted to recruit him to do the same for them. Their letters made clear the high regard that Rory was now held in:

"Your impact on Zizz has impressed us greatly ..."

"We believe you can help us with the challenge of positioning our product better in the marketplace ..."

Rory soon yearned for a normal quiet life, but this was proving a bit difficult for the boy who now had his very own post van delivery every day.

His desire for anonymity was also because his so-called "marketing genius" — the phrase used in any article that featured him — was based on him having overheard someone else. Call it a niggle or a prick of conscience, but the success didn't sit comfortably with Rory and he still waited for the day when the skipping girl from the café would reappear saying "that's my song ... you nicked it."

Rory decided that the best he could do was to quietly let the Zizz campaign run its course. As a result, he gave polite refusals to each of the requests that came in and developed the response that "he wasn't taking on any new clients at the moment." In the back of his mind he was pretty sure he would never do another marketing job. He reckoned that the safest approach was for Zizz to be a one-off and for early retirement to be as far as his marketing career would go.

And then the letter arrived.

Twinkle twinkle Hotel Grimm
Wish your lights would just go dim
Up above us in the town
Always feel you're looking down
Twinkle twinkle Hotel Grimm
Wish your lights would just go dim

Children's Song

5. The impossible challenge

Poised to crumple it up and throw it away, Rory forced himself to look at the letter one last time. The top of the page had the same snarling wolf's head emblem as the now-broken seal from the envelope. The spidery script seemed to have been scratched onto the paper by a sputtering fountain pen.

> Granville Grimm looks forward to receiving Mr Rory McKenna for a meeting at Hotel Grimm on Saturday 1st June at 10.30am precisely. The project for discussion is "Rebranding Hotel Grimm," which Mr McKenna has been chosen to manage.

Rebranding Hotel Grimm? he thought shaking his head for the umpteenth time. He had given up groaning about it because his throat was getting too sore from doing so. *How could anyone successfully come up with a new name and image for something as unspeakably awful and downright dangerous as Hotel Grimm?*

As far as Rory could recall, anyone who had ever stayed there in his lifetime had emerged in a coffin-shaped box, or gone on to die a horrible death elsewhere.

All in all, a delightful place for a holiday, he thought. *How would you advertise that?*

Need to get to your grave that little bit faster? Come and stay at Hotel Grimm!

Ever wanted to disappear and not come back? Try our 2 nights for the price of 1 Special Vanishing Deals!

Whilst the challenge of rebranding Scrab Hill's notorious establishment was a major concern in itself, what presented Rory with his biggest worry was another phrase in the letter.

"… Mr McKenna has been chosen to manage."

What do they mean by "has been chosen?" thought Rory, breaking out in an uncontrollable hot sweat. *Surely it's up to me to choose who I work with … or not?* he despaired.

In the back of his mind, however, Rory knew that this was not the way that things worked with Hotel Grimm. Not only did the place spoil the view like a carbuncle on the landscape, but it cast a shadow over the town in a much more sinister way. The hotel's disastrous record on looking after its guests in recent years, meant that it had become the neighbour that no Aberfintry resident wanted anything to do with.

Given recent stories, Rory knew without a doubt that everyone in the town would agree at the moment, that the only thing worse than going to a meeting at Hotel Grimm would be the possible consequences of not going. The latest edition of *The Chronicle* said it all. Rory could picture it lying on the coffee table downstairs. *"Say "No!" at Your Peril!"* screamed the headline as the story went on to explain that strange and awful things had happened in the last week to two of Aberfintry's tradesmen, who had recently turned down work at Hotel Grimm.

> Experienced electrician Willie Docherty, remains in hospital after connecting a doorbell to the street-lamp grid. "It happened within minutes of me posting Granville Grimm a note to say I wasn't interested in rewiring his freaky hotel," said Willie from his hospital bed. Meanwhile painter and decorator Scott McAndrew, in the bed next to Willie, has just survived being crushed under eighty rolls of wallpaper, which avalanched out of his van. "I was asked to quote a price for decorating that dump and I told them I wasn't interested," said Scott. "I went round to the back of the van and the next thing I knew I was buried under half a ton of paper. That place is pure evil."

Based on the two mens' stories, *The Chronicle* had reached its own conclusion.

> Woe betide the next person to turn down a request to do something there. All you can hope for is that your line of business is not what they need next, up at Hotel Death.

Rory reckoned if he turned down the appointment then he might as well put in a call to the hospital now to tell the nurses to start turning down the sheets and fluffing up the pillows on the bed next to Willie and Scott, in preparation for his arrival. Just as the wording in the letter suggested, there was really no choice for him.

He knew that there were numerous other stories attached to the hotel in the past, and he decided to hunt around the house for some back issues of *The Chronicle* so that he could check them out. He wanted to remind himself of the detail, even though part of him dreaded doing so. Checking with his Mum she waved a vague hand and told him that the old newspapers were all in the kitchen. Unfortunately, it turned out that this was because everything that had once been a newspaper in the house had been used for a papier mâché project of Momo's, and anything that might have given him a useful insight into some of the hotel's recent deeds, had been pulped, shaped, dried and painted and was now hanging in a selection of randomly shaped objects on the pulley. The only copy of *The Chronicle* he could find was an ancient one that his Dad's wellies sat on in the shed. Peering between the muddy stains, he managed to make out a story of a Council meeting that Granville Grimm left in "a foul mood, unhappy about the attitude of councillors to his views on the town's mural". The next day, lightning had struck the Council building resulting in a fire in the room where the meeting had been held. *The Chronicle* concluded that Hotel Grimm's owner appeared to have unnatural powers and was prepared to use them in unpleasant ways.

Try as he might to think of a way of avoiding the appointment he had been given, Rory couldn't come up with one. The thought of what might befall him if he did, seemed to always get in the way. As the inevitability of having to go to Hotel Grimm sank in, something else dawned on Rory.

"It's a punishment!" he said out loud. "Just because I never gave that girl any credit."

Trying to remain positive, he reckoned that he could at least get ready for the meeting about rebranding Hotel Grimm; his best hope being to go there and politely decline their invitation.

Did you mean: **hotel grimm**

No standard web pages containing all your search items were found.

Search engine message

6. Too many dead guests

The first stage of Rory's preparations involved undertaking some background research and he turned to his computer to see what the Internet could offer. He soon found that there was disappointingly little about Hotel Grimm. It was almost as though the search engines refused to handle the name or produce any results. The main reference he did track down was on a website that listed all of the known cable cars in the world. It provided a potted history on where Scrab Hill's own machine had appeared from.

Rory learned that, on returning from the war in 1946 with too many ideas and a large inheritance to spend, Sir Gregory Grimm had set to work having the contraption built that still stood to this day. Within the history of the cable car, there was also a report of a mini avalanche in 1989 on Scrab Hill that had buried three children and their dog while they were out sledging one January afternoon. The unusual movement of the snow that had left the group trapped up to their necks had been blamed on the quivering pylons of the cable car. Given that the cable car had such a strong connection with the Hotel, the finger of blame was pointed at the establishment for nearly taking the lives of some of the town's youngsters.

Rory's Internet search also revealed the obituary of hotel critic, Katy Cribb, who on the day her review of Hotel Grimm was published in 2007, had choked on a chunk of aubergine and died at the very next place she visited. Her review had been scathing to say the least:

> I use the word "dump" advisedly as that appears to be excessively complimentary. If our magazine had a way of awarding minus scores ... Hotel Grimm would surely deserve them all. It is a catastrophically bad experience to cross the threshold, let alone brave staying the night there.

Katy Cribb would now review no more and it seemed that the hotel had somehow managed to serve its own rather extreme judgment on her opinion of it, even after she had left the premises.

Other than that, the best that Rory had got from an hour or two of searching were enough references to suggest that *The Chronicle's* archive located in Aberfintry's library, might provide the best source of information. He also found reference to one book on the hotel. The locally-produced publication was about Hotel Grimm's statues and stone carvings and had been written by Lachlan Stagg. Rory knew that the unfortunate author, who was now missing presumed dead, had been Aberfintry's best attempt at having a local celebrity, before his own Zizz-inspired appearance. Stagg's efforts at gaining as many world records as he could, had given the town much entertainment over the years and helped to put it on the map.

Realizing that newspapers and books needed to be the next port of call, Rory decided to make a journey to the library, although this in itself presented something of a challenge. Given the choice, he tended to spend time playing on his computer or kicking a ball around rather than putting any effort into deciding what to read, let alone ploughing through a book itself. At best, Rory dipped into a few comics, so as he approached the library at the end of a school day, he felt like a fish about to head out of the water. It didn't help to bump into Marnie di Angelo, one of Gracie Goodman's friends as he reached the door.

"Zizz Boy?" she said with a raised eyebrow. "Fancy seeing you here. Just here to read about yourself in the magazines are you?"

Rory mumbled something in response, feeling like a giant spotlight had just been turned on him, and that anyone inside would be staring at him. The only familiar person that Rory spotted, was Bonnie O'Donnell. Thanks to Gordon and Gracie Goodman, Bonnie was known to the whole school as the Worm, short for the Bookworm, as she could usually be found reading in the corner of the playground, so it was no surprise to Rory to find her in here. One of the assistants was lifting down a book for her from a high shelf as Bonnie was in a wheelchair.

"You look a little lost. Can I help you?" said the woman behind the front desk looking up from a pile of books that she was sorting. Her badge said "Mrs Trinder-Kerr. Librarian. Happy to Help."

"Er yes, I need some reference books please," said Rory.

"The reference section is up at the back on the

left," said Mrs Trinder-Kerr pointing to the far corner. "Anything in particular that you're after?"

"I'm doing a little local history project," said Rory, trying hard to remain as vague as he could.

"Well, that narrows it down a bit," said Mrs Trinder-Kerr coming out from behind the desk. "We've got a few books on the area. What is it you are trying to find out?"

Rory hesitated. "Well ... er ... actually ... I was wondering what you have on Hotel Grimm?"

Mrs Trinder-Kerr's helpful face froze momentarily. "We have some information ... I don't often get asked for it," she added, looking strangely at Rory.

"No, I expect not," said Rory deciding not to broadcast the reasons for his research.

Without another word and with a great deal of haste Mrs Trinder-Kerr found him what he was looking for. Returning to her desk, she promptly knocked over the pile of books which she had been sorting and glared across the library at Rory as if implying that he had something to do with her sudden clumsiness. Rory was aware that Bonnie O'Donnell had glanced over at him, but he kept his head lowered and settled himself as best he could at a large table. As he did so, he realized to his embarrassment that the seat he'd chosen was right beside a large poster for his Mum's current exhibition. Rory could hardly look at the title proclaiming "Kitchen Utensils and the Meaning of Life." The picture showed the piece that he knew Momo to be most excited about; it was a metal sieve, entitled "Metal Sieve."

"Why can't she just paint some pictures like proper artists?" his Grandad had asked during one of their regular cups of tea together.

"It's contemporary art," Rory had said, finding himself in the odd position of defending the creative efforts of his mother, which often left him bemused.

"I'm sure your Gran bought her that sieve," said Grandad. "Does that mean there will be some royalties coming my way?"

"Not sure," Rory had said. "I think your claim has a few holes in it." The memory of his awful joke failed to raise a smile as with a mixture of nervousness and curiosity he prepared to leaf through the material Mrs Trinder-Kerr had found for him. The archive took the form of a giant album containing a century's worth of press cuttings from Aberfintry's local paper *The Chronicle*. The front of each issue from the past thirty years sported the name of Derek Goodman, the owner and editor, as well as Gracie and Gordon's dad. He was responsible for the stories about the town, a large proportion of which seemed to be about Hotel Grimm. Prior to that, the name on the articles changed to Hunter Goodman and Sidney Goodman before that. *The Chronicle* had been a family business stretching back through the twentieth century.

As he immersed himself in the archive, Rory found that articles about Hotel Grimm, from as far back as the late 1940s, had a particular flavour to them, leaving no doubt that the paper was no supporter of the establishment.

The most chilling article Rory came across was

one which summarized a list of those who had recently met their end at the hotel over the years. Cheerily entitled "Too Many Dead Guests" it provided a short profile on how six unfortunate people had become ex-guests:

Martin Piggory. Found dead in his pyjamas next to a giant statue of a wolf in the hotel's hallway. It appeared that the elderly, and rather nervous gentleman had been scared to death while on a search for a midnight glass of milk.

Wilma Yeomans. An over-curious antique collector who, it was thought, had stepped over guard rails to investigate an inscription on a suit of armour. The movement had caused its axe-wielding arm to descend, thus rapidly ending her research.

Sir Ivan Clinton. The pre-pack salad tycoon drowned in Sir Gregory Grimm's famously giant bath in the hotel's deluxe suite when his big toe had become stuck in one of the taps, rendering him unable to lean forward to turn the other tap off.

Davina Aitken. Poisoned while on the premises. The hotel had vigorously denied any connection between their kitchens and the death. Investigations revealed that Aitken was a fungi collector who had wrongly identified, and then eaten, a handful of Aberfintry's notorious and deadly pink skullcap toadstools.

Peter Pendreich. A sporting enthusiast died when it seemed that a playful attempt to lasso his bedroom's chandelier with his dressing-gown cord had ended in a bizarre combination of strangulation and electrocution.

Donald Burnside. Accidentally shot himself. The phone beside his bed had rung with the alarm call from hotel reception that he had requested. Unfortunately, in his sleepy state, instead of the receiver, he picked up the pistol he always kept on his bedside table.

The hotel had denied any wrongdoing in any of these incidents, describing each as an unfortunate accident, and claiming that it had since taken appropriate action: removing the wolf statue, replacing the bath taps, putting signs up about the dangers of lassos and local fungi, and asking guests to leave firearms in the hotel safe. It remained adamant that these were a series of accidents.

The catalogue of catastrophes was never-ending. Flicking through the archive Rory spotted headlines about a rock fall that had nearly flattened a school picnic, a six-foot long python kept as a pet in the hotel, which had ended up under a guest's pillow, and a fire that had resulted in the dramatic rescue of an American guest by a member of staff. As far as he could see, there was not a single positive story about the hotel.

As he worked his way through the album, Rory also found *The Chronicle's* efforts to counter the negative stories of Hotel Grimm. He came across a picture of the library itself in the article about the unveiling of the statue of Lachlan Stagg. The public event ended months of campaigning to raise funds to pay for the creation of a feature that, the paper said, "would commemorate someone that the town could be proud of in contrast to the unwanted residents of Scrab Hill."

The fact that Hotel Grimm was considered not just a dangerous but also a downright sinister place increased after the experience of Aberfintry resident, Bella Valentine. She had been employed as a cleaner at the hotel two years previously, and had lasted all of two weeks. Even that short experience had been enough to establish her new career as the official voice on what life was like inside the hotel. Looking through the archive, Rory couldn't help wondering why Bella would have taken the job in the first place, given the fear and loathing surrounding the hotel. But the more he read the more he saw that it had been a good career move since she seemed to get a feature in every couple of weeks as *The Chronicle* kept coming up with new angles about her "horrifying experience." It seemed as though Bella Valentine had had her own rebranding. Every time a photo of her appeared it was accompanied by the caption of "Hotel Grimm Survivor."

Bella was thorough in her analysis that everything about the hotel was at best bad, and at worst downright evil. It went from the cable car — "The man that runs it is a funny one and I swear that cable car is going to just fall off those wires some day" — moved on to the hotel itself — "I hardly want to think about what hideous things lurk within its walls" — and got personal about Granville Grimm — "the man looms around like some giant brooding ogre."

"Whatcha reading, Zizz man?" said a voice, interrupting Rory from Bella Valentine's account. He looked up to find Max Fletcher, one of Gordon Goodman's cronies, standing by his table. Rory couldn't help but lean over the book he was looking at to try and shield its contents from Fletcher. "Er … nothing much … just doing … just doing a local history project."

"Looks like you want it to be top secret," said Fletcher, sidling closer to Rory and twisting his head to see more clearly. His eyes narrowed as they flickered around the archive's pages. As it dawned on him what he was looking at, he pulled back sharply.

"Local history?" he hissed, lowering his voice and glancing left and right as if checking if anyone was watching them. "They say that fizzy drinks are bad for your health, Zizz Boy.... but it's your choice of reading material you should be careful about."

Fletcher turned away and Rory tried to concentrate again on the job in hand. He felt even more self-conscious now and glancing up he saw Max Fletcher and Marnie di Angelo heading out of the door together a few minutes later, looking over at him as they did. Relaxing a little he turned back with a sigh to *The Chronicle* archive.

The only thing Bella Valentine was remotely complimentary about was the kitchen. "I will give you one thing — it is so clean, it is a work of art, although even there I could swear I once caught a glimpse of a rat."

Her account finished with these chilling words:

There are strange and dangerous creatures within the walls; a poltergeist or some such meddlesome creature. That is the only way to explain the way that books move around in the library from one hour to the next. Worst of all, and the reason why I shall never set foot in the place again, is that something lives and lurks in one of the corridors. It tried to attack me. It got so close that its breath echoed in my ears and its spittle rained on my head. There was a clanking sound from it that was like the devil rattling the gates of heaven trying to get in. Fortunately, I was just too fast for it, otherwise I might never have walked Aberfintry's streets again.

The photo of Bella that *The Chronicle* used, made you wonder why the mysterious beast hadn't stopped in its tracks and run in the opposite direction. Bella's fiercesome scowl and the fact that she probably took up most of any corridor would have made her an alarming sight for even the most discerning monster, Rory reckoned.

The Chronicle had often looked for a comment from PC Malky Mackay whenever something awful had happened, but all they seemed to have got from the policeman was that the incidents were being looked into, or that there appeared to be no evidence of any wrongdoing. There certainly never seemed to be any police backing for the paper's dislike of the place.

Having grown up with an understanding that Hotel Grimm's sinister reputation made it a place to avoid, Rory now saw a pattern emerging that he had been unaware of before. *The Chronicle* seemed to suggest that there was a starting point for the hotel's notoriety, which was linked to particular events.

"Since the events of 1948, the Hotel has been a place to avoid …"
"The tragedy of 1948 was the catalyst for things beginning to go wrong."
"That awful night in 1948 set the tone for years to come …"

Rory began to flick through pages to establish just what had happened all those years ago.

"We're closing." The voice cut into the weird world that he was reading about. Mrs Trinder-Kerr was standing behind him, arms crossed and nose scrunched as though a bad smell had lodged there.

As he stepped outside, he felt that he had more questions than answers. He sat at the base of the Lachlan Stagg statue that he had read about a few minutes before. Rory had walked past it countless times but never paid much attention, so it was with a fresh pair of eyes that he looked more closely at the figure. Cast in bronze, it was of a life-size, older man clad in a tweed suit with plus fours. There was an intense look in his eyes and wild hair going in every direction. The statue was detailed enough that the top of its left ear even had a deep notch missing. With one hand raised and a pointing finger, the figure appeared poised for action, as though it had just had an idea and was about to leap down and carry on where the real Lachlan Stagg had left off. Rory noticed for the first time that there was an inscription carved into the concrete base.

LACHLAN STAGG

ABERFINTRY'S VERY OWN RECORD HOLDER
AN EXAMPLE TO US ALL OF HOW TO MAKE YOUR MARK

Below this, a small plaque stated:

THE STATUE OF LACHLAN STAGG AND THE ABERFINTRY MURAL WERE MADE POSSIBLE WITH THE SUPPORT OF THE CHRONICLE AND THE PEOPLE OF ABERFINTRY, AS AN EXPRESSION OF THE POSITIVE FEATURES OF THIS TOWN.

Rory glanced beyond the statue to the mural on the adjacent wall. Running for fully ten metres, it formed a giant map of Aberfintry, picking out some of the main features of the town; the High Street, the library, the school, the river, the park and the gallery with people sitting outside its café and the statue itself. It was full of life and colour with little matchstick figures in the streets and bright front doors on the houses. Rory remembered that *The Chronicle* had made a very public event of the mural's creation, trying to unite everyone in a celebration of the town. They had even involved most of the classes in the primary and secondary schools in painting bits of it, but they had been very clear about one aspect. On either side of Scrab Hill the sky was bathed in blue, but the hilltop itself was covered with cloud obliterating any sign of Hotel Grimm. *The Chronicle* had been explicit that the hotel was not to be included. Rory couldn't help but wonder what it was in 1948 that had led to the need for Hotel Grimm to be hidden in the clouds.

A door shutting behind him broke his train of thought. Rory looked around to find Bonnie O'Donnell emerging from the library just ahead of Mrs Trinder-Kerr, who locked the door as she left. Out of the corner of his eye, Rory thought he saw Bonnie pause as if considering whether to come over and speak to him. Sensing this and not wanting his interest in Hotel Grimm to spark off any further problems, Rory looked away.

Back in the comfort of his bedroom, pulling the tab on a can of Zizz to cheer himself up Rory remembered that even though it hadn't given him all the answers, he had now followed through the first stage of his plan by going to the library. Step two would involve a trip to Boglehole Road.

There was a young man called Tim
Who most thought incredibly dim
He proved it one day
By losing his way
And asking directions at Grimm

Limerick

7. Boglehole Road

Rory put his key in the lock and his shoulder to the door of 47, Boglehole Road, thumping it open as he always did.

"It's me," he shouted as he pushed it closed again.

Hearing no response, he put his head round the first door on the left. The room was now a combination of living room, bedroom and kitchen since his Grandad had begun to struggle with the steep stairs of the house.

Today, as on most days, Grandad was in his favourite seat, his legs invisible beneath a tartan blanket and the pages of the newspaper scattered around. He was sound asleep.

Rory quite liked the idea of having everything in one room: comfy seat, TV, toaster, kettle, bed, snacks on hand and no need to ever move too far to do anything. He knew though that his Grandad hated the fact that he could no longer get to parts of his own house.

The room displayed much of Grandad's life through a patchwork of framed photos: holiday pictures of Rory's Gran who had died many years before; some of his Mum throughout her childhood; and one of Grandad at work in Aberfintry's park, his bald head nut brown from days of summer gardening. The sleeping figure in the armchair now had the pasty look of someone who had not crossed the doorstep for some time.

By the window was the stand with his Grandad's telescope, which the old man could no longer use because of his failing eyesight. Rory often spent time looking through it, but today the view towards Scrab Hill was only an unwelcome reminder of his imminent appointment.

Rory flopped on to the settee, frustrated that he would have to wait for any helpful conversation with Grandad. Boglehole Road had become a great place to come to if he had something on his mind, particularly as his mum and dad were so busy with their own activities.

"I might not have the legs to run a race any more but I've got two great lugs for listening," Grandad would often say. In previous years, much of their time was spent in the workshop at the bottom of the path, where there was an old armchair in which he would sit as Grandad pottered away on cuttings or seeds for the garden. The armchair was pushed against a door, which Rory had only ever seen padlocked, and he had given up asking what was in there. "My wee hidey hole," was as much explanation as his Grandad had ever given.

It was a good two or three years now since Rory had been down to the workshop because Grandad was now inside the house and their activities had changed as a result.

"Right it's whist this week. A great wee card game, but you'll need to concentrate," he'd say shuffling the pack with still-nimble fingers.

Recently, Rory's efforts to teach his Grandad how to text had exasperated the old man.

"Would you not just be quicker talking to folk, Rory?" Rory thought it was funny that the man whose fingers could fly across the buttons and keys of an accordion and produce such fantastic music could fail to key in "Hi Rory it's Gdad" to a mobile phone.

"That's because I'm making proper music," said Grandad defensively, "not setting off some daft ring tone."

In recent times, Rory's favourite thing to do at Boglehole Road was to look through the black metal box with the clasp and padlock, that Grandad called his "wee treasure chest." No matter how often Rory looked in it, he always found something he hadn't noticed before; a button from an army uniform, a rabbit's foot, or a dog-eared sepia photo of Grandad in a suit on an ancient-looking bike.

"What's this?" Rory would ask and within minutes he was transported to another time and place by stories of the past.

Today, however, was going to be one of the increasingly common days when Rory sat in silence and then slipped away unnoticed.

Looking for something to distract him, Rory reached over for a recent copy of *The Chronicle* sitting on the coffee table. The headline read "Sheep left cold by Grimm's Hill." The front page article described how farmer Angus Robb's anger that his sheep grazing on Scrab Hill were producing a low yield of wool. "You'd be lucky to get a balaclava out of each of them," said the farmer. The paper concluded that "even the hill was now affected by the hotel's presence."

Rory sighed. With every story he read about Hotel Grimm he seemed to hear the clunk of another nail being driven into his own coffin. Inside the paper he found a special "Memorial Edition" supplement entitled "Lachlan Stagg. Aberfintry's own Record Breaker. The Legacy lives on."

Opening it up, Rory found a biography of the man, born and bred in Aberfintry, whose life had been dedicated to achieving as many world records as he could. By the time his record-breaking career was cut short, he had amassed a remarkable fifty-nine of them, one for every year of his life. "World records require imagination, creativity and discipline," Stagg was quoted as saying. "It's not just achieving them, it's setting them at a level where you are likely to hold on to them."

As Rory read on, he discovered that Stagg had begun early, gaining his first record at the age of eleven with a twenty-six foot tall house of cards. The picture of this was alongside others of Stagg in the act of claiming various records. There was one of Stagg emerging rather hot and considerably thinner about the face than usual, as the result of spending four consecutive, record-breaking weeks in a gas mask, and another with his arms aloft, bedecked with medals after winning the annual Scrab Hill Race for the sixth time in a row. This feat had never been equalled as the event was stopped for safety fears after a landslide narrowly missed competitors. *The Chronicle* claimed that the hotel's subterranean work on a new wine cellar was to blame.

Rory read on about Lachlan Stagg's knack of turning misfortune into achievement, best illustrated by the River Fintry fly-fishing competition, when a wayward cast led the hook on his line to whizz past his head and gouge a chunk out of his left ear. Ten minutes later, the unplanned-for bait ended up landing the biggest fish ever caught in the River Fintry.

Down one side of the page, were listed Stagg's record-breaking collection of qualifications amassed throughout his life; lawyer, architect, pilot, plumber, chef, acupuncturist, judo master, Russian teacher, ski instructor and tiger tamer to name but a few.

These skills often led to yet more records. For example, as a chef, when together with Ramsay Sandilands, a local cooking enthusiast, he created the largest pancake ever made. Stagg balanced an enormous pan on the roundabout in the local park and provided the whole town with breakfast.

As time went on, and Stagg's list of achievements grew, he spotted the one record that he was keenest to achieve. He wanted to become the world record holder for the person with the most world records. But it was not to be. Stagg even had a connection with Hotel Grimm, as the author of a book about the stonecarvings and gargoyles there, but it was this publication that was linked to his untimely demise. Following three nights of heavy rain, Stagg's fishing gear was found by the side of the swollen River Fintry. His hat and one wader were discovered far downstream and, after much fruitless searching, the only conclusion was that Stagg had drowned in pursuit of one of his favourite pastimes. The fact that this tragic event had taken place on the day his book was launched was enough for people to believe that Hotel Grimm had robbed the town of its favourite son.

Another heart-warming story, thought Rory casting the paper aside. Grandad grunted but failed to stir any further. Deciding that today was not the day to find wise words at Boglehole Road, Rory tiptoed out, leaving a note to say he had dropped in, but without mentioning his increasingly imminent appointment.

Trudging home and lost in his thoughts, Rory didn't notice the bike pulling up beside him at first. "Boo," said a voice gently beside him. Startled, Rory turned to find PC Mackay beside him. It hurt Rory's neck to talk to Aberfintry's police officer. At 6 feet 5 inches tall he towered above most things. Fortunately he often squatted down to chat, his long legs bending like a grasshopper's to get low enough for a face to face conversation.

"You look a bit pre-occupied," said Malky.

"Supppose so," said Rory.

"Been to see your Grandad?" asked the policeman, now pushing his bike and taking a measured stride to fit in with Rory's slow walk.

"Yeah, but he was snoozing so it was a wasted trip."

"Aye, he seems to be sleeping more these days," said Malky.

Rory said nothing prompting Malky to look at him. "You okay, Rory? You seem a bit low."

"I was wanting to ask my Grandad about something but I timed it wrong."

"Can I help?" asked Malky.

Rory thought for a second and then threw caution to the wind. "If you knew someone who was planning to go up to Hotel Grimm would you be concerned?"

Malky's eyebrows raised momentarily. He nodded slowly and looked thoughtful. "Not if he had told someone he was going and when he expected to be back … and that he didn't do anything daft when he was up there," said Malky. "I know a lot of other people in this town would have a very different opinion, but that's mine."

"But what about its reputation?" asked Rory.

"You don't get harmed by a reputation. You get harmed by dangerous people or by taking silly risks. There are none of the first up there, so tell your friend to avoid the second and they'll be okay."

Rory nodded. "This um … friend, was talking of going up there on Saturday morning for about three hours, I think."

Malky gave a brief nod and then pointed left. "I have to go this way," he said. "Good to see you again, Rory. Tell your friend to take care now," he added looking back over his shoulder.

With a day to go, Rory found his thoughts taken up more and more with what Saturday morning might bring, so much so that he couldn't face doing some of the things that were part of normal everyday life for him. The other lads looked a bit bemused as he turned down a game of playground football and took himself off.

"Come on, Rory ..."

"Yeah what's up, Zizz Boy?"

"Got some new prize-winning slogan on your mind?"

Instead, Rory found a quiet corner to sit and read some of the scribbled notes he had made from his shift in the library, which did little other than depress him and provide further anxiety about the weekend's appointment. To make matters worse he opened his lunchbox to find that Momo had mistaken it for one of her craft containers. It was packed it with playdough, straws and tubes of glitter.

"I saw you in the library the other day." Rory was interrupted from thoughts of his rumbling stomach. Bonnie O'Donnell was sitting in front of him having made her way over from her usual reading spot by the trees at the far side of the playground.

"Yeah, I saw you too," said Rory, trying not to make it obvious that he was clutching his notes together to keep them hidden from view.

"Haven't seen you in there before," said Bonnie.

"No ... probably not," replied Rory, trying not to get drawn into anything.

"Reference books?" Bonnie asked with a half smile.

"Yeah ... yeah, that's right," said Rory.

"I couldn't help noticing *which* reference books you were after ... and Mrs Trinder-Kerr confirmed it."

Rory said nothing.

"Oh come on, Rory," said Bonnie after a pause.

"What were you doing checking out information on Hotel Grimm?"

Rory shrugged.

"People generally only take an interest in that place if they absolutely have to. I'm guessing you're in that camp?"

Rory wanted to blurt out everything, but was too frightened even to hear himself say what he was getting into. He looked away from Bonnie into the distance at the other boys kicking a ball about. Beyond them there was the playground fence, a line of houses and then the stark silhouette of Scrab Hill and Hotel Grimm.

Rory said nothing.

"Fair enough," she continued, "but if you ask me, that big archive of press cuttings is amazing, and if ... just if ... you happened to be taking an interest in the hotel, let me know."

With that, Bonnie's electric wheelchair buzzed into action. She spun round and headed away.

8. Ramsay and the rats

His journey had started with a surprise. Opening the front door he had nearly stood on a package sitting on the step. A short note was taped to the box.

> *I'm guessing you might need these soon.*
> *Let me know how you get on.*
> *Bonnie*

Inside he found a pair of binoculars. Rory was very taken aback that Bonnie was prepared to communicate with him at all, let alone willing to trust him with such great-looking equipment. His unwillingness to talk to her in the playground had obviously not put her off. It felt good that someone was taking an interest and so it was with more of a spring in his step that he had set off.

Beads of sweat were beginning to surface on Rory's forehead as, three quarters of an hour later, he reached the huge flat rock ledge that jutted out like a giant step on Scrab Hill, a short distance below the hotel.

Stopping for a rest he settled himself with his feet dangling over the edge and caught his breath as he surveyed the landscape below. He had never realized what a fantastic view there was from here. Rory could see how Aberfintry nestled in a landscape of green rolling hills with the sparkling ribbon of the River Fintry threading through it. From the town, it seemed that all you saw was the hill topped by the dark monstrosity of Hotel Grimm. Up on the hill itself and looking the other way, this was no longer a problem. Rory could see for miles and miles.

"Why don't people come up here more often?" he thought to himself as he took in the sweeping view. Just then a sharp gust of cold wind made him shiver and he shuddered as it hummed and moaned in the cable car wires above his head. He looked upwards to see the silhouette of Hotel Grimm and answered his own question.

Whilst the view from the ledge was spectacular, the rock formation had its own eyesore. A wrecked building stood at one end, within the half cave created by a massive overhang of rock. Curtain tatters hung in the shabby window frames, a clutter of furniture had been shovelled into a heap at one end, and there were stained and dried-out fish tanks piled around.

Turning away, Rory pulled out Bonnie's binoculars and focused on the town below, scanning his way through the streets. It wasn't long before he had picked out his own house and bedroom window. He wondered if he should have left some kind of a note explaining about his trip up Scrab Hill and everything that had led up to it.

As he looked a familiar car came into view, crawling painfully slowly with its Learner Driver sign on top. He imagined his father inside with a perspiring student struggling to master the basics of being behind the wheel. He turned his attention towards the edge of the town, resting eventually on the cable car station at the foot of Scrab Hill. There was movement as a hunched figure trudged round the outside of the building. Rory knew straightaway that it must be Stobo, the hermit-like mechanic who was solely responsible for the fact that the cable car was still in working condition. Even from this distance, Rory could see that he was wearing overalls and heavy boots, his squat figure topped off with a flat cap. Occasionally, Stobo appeared in town dressed like this, moving through the streets like some odd beetle that had briefly emerged into daylight before discovering that it wanted to retreat under a rock.

As Stobo disappeared back inside the cable car station, Rory returned the binoculars to his backpack and pulled out a snack, deciding to get a boost of energy before the final bit of the climb. He took a big bite out of a banana and flicked the ring-pull on a can of Zizz.

"Morning."

Rory jumped at the sound of a voice nearby, a large lump of banana lodging in his throat as he did so. Coughing and choking, he jerked around, knocking over his drink, but he couldn't see where the greeting had come from.

"Not speaking then?"

Rory's eyes flickered around the ledge but again he failed to identify the source.

"I can't see you," he said swallowing hard.

"Over here," said the voice.

Rory turned to a pile of boulders close to the derelict building. A small whiskery man in a hairy coat and an equally hairy pointed hat was perched on a rock watching him with a thin smile. He was caressing a large rat and had two more sitting on either shoulder. As Rory watched, other rats poked their heads out from his pockets and from behind his back, as if to see who the man was talking to.

Rory had heard of dog owners looking like their dogs, but the man in front of him seemed to have acquired many of the characteristics of the rats. His long sharp nose twitched and sniffed the air in the same quick, jerky manner, and he had whiskers on his cheeks and tiny round pink ears. Rory half-expected him to stand up and reveal a ropey tail flapping below the hem of his unusual coat. With so many rats crawling over the little man, Rory tried hard not to feel squeamish, and his unease was soon spotted.

"What's the matter?" said the man pointedly.

Rory looked away in silent embarrassed response.

"You seem to be staring at me — it's rude," the man snapped.

"It's just ... em ... I'm just not used to seeing rats ... I mean, I've never seen so many at one time," said Rory.

"Oh, here we go. I thought, since you had at least made the effort to come up the hill, that you might think a little differently from that lot down in the town," snipped the man.

"I'm sorry. I didn't mean to offend you, Mr ...?" Rory left the question hanging in the hope that he could change the subject.

The man stood up and did a theatrical bow removing his hairy hat and revealing the wispy top of a balding head. “Ramsay Sandilands at your service,” he declared.

“I’m Rory…Rory McKenna. I live down there,” he said nodding at Aberfintry. The man inclined his head as if to note that this was not new information. “Do you live near here?” Rory added.

“I have a room at the hotel,” said the man. “I work there.”

“I suppose your friends are quite at home there then?” asked Rory nodding towards the rats.

The atmosphere frosted over again as Ramsay pulled himself upright. “Oh and why would that be? What are you implying might I ask?”

“Well rats aren’t normally too fussy about where they live, are they?” said Rory aware that he might be stepping into hot water. Ramsay gathered his coat around himself and herded the rats closer to him in a protective bundle.

“Here we go, boys…same old attitudes all over again. Just as I suspected.” A dozen pink noses twitched up at him as he spoke. Ramsay sighed. “People get so hysterical. It’s pathetic. You’ve all got it wrong you know, Rory McKenna,” he said.

“Are you trying to say that rats get a bad press?” Rory asked incredulously.

“Bad press? Bad press?!” said Ramsay squeaking in an ever higher voice. “Oh let me see what words would normally be used to describe rats? Filthy … scavenging … disease-carrying … vermin …”

“Um … are they not all true?” said Rory tentatively.

Ramsay puffed his thin frame out to give importance to his statement. “Rats are naturally clean animals, soiled only by man’s environment.”

Rory would often let things pass if they seemed too much trouble, but he felt quite strongly about this one. "Correct me if I'm wrong," he said. "But rats don't exactly have a great reputation in relation to the human population, do they?"

Ramsay looked away and mumbled something about the "little bubonic plague episode."

"Little bubonic plague episode!" said Rory. "I've heard of "putting a positive spin on things" but that's a bit rich. If I remember my school project correctly, about twenty-five million people died because of it!"

Ramsay hopped off his rock in agitation.

"It wasn't the rats that carried the disease it was fleas! They just happened to travel about on rats. The rats were innocent and have taken the blame for too long."

As Ramsay came closer, Rory noticed that his hairy coat sported a campaign lapel badge. The logo of a silhouette of a rat sported the message, "We didn't do it!" Ramsay's face broke into a lopsided grin. "Maybe we need some marketing genius to help us improve our profile. Do you happen to know one?"

Rory frowned at Ramsay's knowledge of his reputation as the little man continued. "Talking of disasters and death … I believe that you're up here for a big meeting at Hotel Grimm?"

"How do you know what I'm up here for?" said Rory, perplexed that halfway up a hillside a small whiskery man with pockets full of rodents knew the contents of his diary.

Ramsay tapped his nose with a long pink finger.

"I work there remember," he said with a nod towards the mist-shrouded hilltop. "It's time for some change and you are thought to be the man for the job. You've even brought evidence of the brilliant mind that's going to help them," he said pointing to Rory's can of Zizz. "It's a rare thing to see a visitor coming to the hotel these days." Ramsay smiled revealing sharp pointed teeth. "The Grimm's guest book does have an unfashionably high and rather off-putting body count."

"So I've read," said Rory. "So what is the story? What makes it such an evil place?"

"Evil?" said Ramsay in derision. He started laughing and as he did so the rats began squeaking uncontrollably. "I do apologise," he said after taking some time to compose himself and his pets. "That was extremely rude of me. Disorganized it may be. Grubby in places it certainly is —although not in my part of the building. Evil it is most certainly not!"

"So what about the small matter of dead guests, poltergeists and beasts?" asked Rory.

"There has been a run of … misfortune," said Ramsay seeming to choose the word carefully.

"Misfortune?" said Rory. "It certainly is a bit unlucky if you're one of the ones who didn't make it out alive. Isn't there more to it than that?"

"Well …," said Ramsay, pondering before speaking again. "Some would say that the misfortune is a direct result of the Curse of the Stonemason."

"Curse … what curse?" asked Rory.

Ramsay's eyes narrowed. "You seem a little bit unprepared for your meeting if the Curse of the

Stonemason is news to you. You'll see some signs of it if you go a little further on. You can't miss the wolf waiting to greet you as you approach the front door."

Rory opened his mouth to speak but was cut off before he could ask for further explanation.

"Much as I would love to sit here and tell stories, it really is time I departed." Ramsay pulled a watch from the depths of his coat. A dozen noses twitched up at him in anticipation. "Boys, we must be off", he said pulling his coat together. "You must excuse me," said Ramsay addressing Rory. "I have something to take out of the oven."

Rory was trying to imagine what this straggly man in a hairy coat with a rat hanging from every limb might be about to remove from an oven. Then it occurred to him where he had read the name Ramsay Sandilands in the last few days.

"You're the pancake man! You did the world record with Lachlan Stagg. I remember now."

Ramsay gave a slow nod, clearly pleased at being recognised. "That is I," he said. "And now I am the chef at Hotel Grimm."

"So what's in the oven?" asked Rory trying to hide his discomfort at the rat owner's revelation.

Ramsay pulled himself up proudly. "Today we have Broccoli and Cheese soup followed by Shepherd's Pie, with Summer Fruits Pavlova to finish. I would humbly suggest that it is likely to be some of the finest food you have eaten in a long time."

Rory couldn't help wondering whether Shepherd's Pie made at Hotel Grimm would actually have bits of shepherds in it.

"Well I hope to have the pleasure some time," he said as politely as he could.

Ramsay made a theatrical closing bow.

"I do wish you all the very best with your meeting," he said. "A genius is what is required. Let us hope you are the one."

Watching Ramsay skip his way through the rocks and disappear Rory forgot for a moment why he was perched on the side of Scrab Hill, and then with a start and a glance at his watch he realized that he had just twenty minutes to get up to the hotel for his appointment. Packing up and throwing on his backpack, Rory set off at a fast pace, fearful of the consequences if he were to turn up late. Thanks to Ramsay Sandilands, he was now feeling even more apprehensive with the prospect of an imminent encounter with a wolf and a curse.

Just above the ledge he passed the upper cable car station. The eerie whistling of the wind in the empty building made him pick up speed. Onwards, upwards and as quickly as the rough stony surface would allow, Rory finally puffed his way around a large boulder and stopped in his tracks. He was only about thirty metres from the hotel, the last bit of the path being formed by huge, jagged slabs of slate zig-zagging up to the front door. In front of him, lying on its side at edge of the path, was an enormous snarling wolf carved in stone in the act of leaping on some unseen prey. The fearsome creature's head reminded Rory of the emblem on the letter that had commanded him to attend the meeting in the first place.

It seemed an odd place for the statue to be, almost as though it had been discarded there. Rory stepped closer. It occurred to him that among the deaths he had read about, one involved an elderly guest being scared to death by a wolf statue. Whatever the story was, the statue was magnificent. Despite being carved in stone, the fur appeared to have a soft texture, while the ferocious head was too life-like for comfort, even though the lolling tongue and some of the teeth had broken off. Rory was clear now about the wolf mentioned by Ramsay Sandilands, but he was none the wiser about the Curse of the Stonemason.

The creak of rusty chains distracted him for a moment, and Rory looked up to see a battered wooden sign, on which he could just make out the wording: "Hotel Grimm. Aberfintry's Finest."

Rory swallowed hard as he began to walk up the steps that led to a vast wooden door. By the time he reached the black stone walls it was set into, he seemed to have stepped into deep shadow and a shiver passed through him. Above him, frozen in stone, was a fearsome leering gargoyle that looked down and mocked him as he stood on the top step. The enormous iron door knocker, was another wolf's head and Rory toyed with the idea of running straight back down the hill, diving through his front door and hiding under his duvet. Then he remembered the one fear that was greater than being here. Not being here. What would happen to him if he didn't turn up?

With an air of resignation he stretched up, heaving the giant wolf's head upwards, before letting it thump down into the wood in the centre of the door. The sound echoed and then faded to silence. A slow shuffling sound and some hacking coughs began and gradually became louder. Eventually, a tiny wooden hatch in the door shot open.

"GO AWAY!" snapped a voice and the hatch slammed shut again.

I think that they need to work on their customer relations for a start, thought Rory.

He raised his hand again, but before he could even reach the knocker, the hatch flew open once more.

"DIDN'T YOU HEAR ME?" squawked a grumpy voice. "GO AWAY!"

"But I have an appointment with Granville Grimm," Rory stuttered.

There was a pause and some grumbling and mumbling from behind the door. After a short silence, there was a slow creak and the front door of Hotel Grimm opened.

Beware of Mr Granville Grimm, the
madman on Scrab Hill
He'll know if you're not listening, so start by
sitting still.
He can curse you with one look so if you
want to live,
You'd better do just as he says, and full
attention give.

*Local cautionary tale to encourage
children to behave*

9. Granville Grimm

For the briefest of moments, daylight revealed the grubby stone-clad hallway as Rory stepped through the front door of Hotel Grimm. He caught a glimpse of fur and teeth from some dilapidated, stuffed animal heads on the wall, but before he could make out any more detail there was a thunderous thud as the door closed and he was consumed by darkness, leaving him in no doubt that he was inside Hotel Grimm for the foreseeable future.

Rory blinked hard, his eyes desperately seeking out some light source, however faint. Gradually a glimmer from a low wattage light bulb, and a crack of light from between two curtains began to help him. As his eyes fought to make sense of anything in the gloom, the faintest detail of carpets, curtains, paintings, pillars and a marble staircase began to emerge.

As his eyes worked overtime, his ears also got to work. He could hear a whistling draught, an occasional drip, a distant hinge creaking and what sounded horribly like the pattering of a small animal's feet. Rory shook his head sharply as if to dispel the sounds and the images they were creating in his mind. At the same time, the smell of damp made his nose wrinkle uncontrollably.

"Hurry up!" barked the rude little man. His shadowy figure was fast disappearing down the dim hallway. Frightened of being left on his own, Rory set off.

but on his first step, something squidged under his foot. He recoiled as he walked on, desperately trying not to think of what it might have been.

There were enough coughs ahead to let Rory know that he was still heading in the right direction, and as he rounded a corner in haste, he thumped straight into the man who was now standing wheezing against a doorpost.

"Oof … sorry," spluttered Rory.

"HOO HA!" The noise erupted right beside him as the man cleared his throat and nose at the same time with the sound of a dredger scraping the life out of the bottom of a pond. Rory's stomach churned as he remembered standing in something a few moments before.

As the man grunted and limped off again, Rory couldn't help but think that any potential guest at Hotel Grimm would already have turned round, headed off at top speed and made alternative arrangements for the night. Occasionally, the man jerked round and managed to seem annoyed to find Rory still there, at the same time as telling him to hurry up. Rory quickly got the impression that there was little that he would be able to do right in the grumpy man's eyes.

After a maze of twisting and turning corridors, Rory was ushered into a cavernous room, poorly lit by a couple of meagre bulbs that failed to cast light into the far corners. Rory decided that he probably didn't want to see into them anyway for fear of what might be lurking there.

All around the room, dark wood panelling covered the walls, while once gilt-framed gloomy portraits of even gloomier-looking men frowned down from all around. Only the whites of their eyes and their starched collars provided the slightest suggestion of light in each picture.

Velvet curtains hung limply at every window, some in tatters, which Rory concluded was probably due to the flock of giant moths that was fluttering around, that looked as if it might have been feeding on the fabric for generations.

Had it been blazing, a fire under the enormous mantlepiece would have brought life and light to the room. Instead a few unconvincing embers glowed feebly as if about to give up the ghost.

"Sit there!" barked the man, shoving Rory towards a giant high-backed throne-like seat at one end of a table so enormously long that it seemed a plane could land on it.

A gigantic candelabra like a twisted tree was topped by three yellowing candles which were now unlit. Wax had dribbled and hardened to form a fantastic sculpture over time, which in the half-light resembled a hand pointing back out of the door, suggesting the quickest escape route.

Rory had the sensation that he was being silently laughed at by the manically laughing faces carved into the wooden back of his seat. It was only after gazing round the room that he realized that a brooding figure was seated in silence at the distant end of the table. Rory made out a furrowed forehead, topped with wild, unruly hair. The man sat motionless apart from the slow movement of one finger twizzling a particularly long lock of hair around and around and around.

As if a bit had been formed from the rocky side of Scrab Hill, the man's face appeared solid, craggy and expressionless. Rory could make out few other features.

"Good morning and thank you for coming."

The soft and polite voice which emerged from the hulking figure made Rory double-take to check where the sound had actually come from.

"Er … no problem," he said, caught off guard. *No problem? No problem?* his own thoughts screamed back at him.

"I am Granville Grimm and am pleased to welcome you here," said the man with the faintest of waves of his hand. "Thank you for agreeing to assist me with my project."

"Er … actually I was hoping we could chat about that," said Rory. "I'm not really …"

Oblivious to Rory's faltering protest, the hotel owner continued. "I need some help and I believe you are the person to provide it. I am only too well aware that the public perception of what we offer here is not … shall we say *favourable* at times."

That's the understatement of the year, thought Rory picturing the screaming headlines in *The Chronicle* that spelled out death and evil in equal measure.

"I'm not sure I'm …" stuttered Rory.

"What I want here is … how can I best describe it?" interrupted Granville Grimm searching for the right words. "What I want is to be … functioning properly again."

Rory looked at the man and found himself wondering if he was talking about the business of the hotel or about himself. For all of his politeness, Granville Grimm"s low, saddened tones presented him as a very melancholic man.

"I am not looking for the high levels of success and achievement you have gained for Zizz Cola," he continued in his low voice. "I just want people to view us in a different light."

Rory stopped himself from saying "...and presumably to have a few guests that check out in the normal fashion by just handing their key back."

Granville Grimm's softly spoken voice and his deliberate choice of words somehow made the idea of changing the hotel's image and getting people back through the door sound like a straightforward project. Rory had to remind himself that this was Hotel Grimm which, as he had just learned, had its very own curse. From the hotel owner's silence it appeared that Rory was now expected to begin to present his thoughts on the situation.

Rory cleared his throat and chose his words carefully. "I think I understand what you want. I don't mean to be pessimistic but ... er ... there are rather a lot of ... er ... large obstacles in the way of success."

There was silence from the other end of the table. Feeling increasingly nervous, Rory blundered on. "I mean it's not just the issue of how you are viewed down in the town. Aren't there some deeper issues that are causing problems here?"

"Do forgive me, but I'm unsure what you mean," said Granville Grimm sounding slightly baffled.

"I mean that no matter what you do to try to change things here, could there be something working against you?" said Rory.

"Go on," said Granville Grimm.

Rory took a deep breath. "I mean The Curse of the Stonemason," he said.

At that moment the stuttering conversation dried up completely and the room seemed to freeze over.

"I want no mention of that." The tone in Granville Grimm's voice chilled the atmosphere still further.

"No of course…." said Rory.

Granville Grimm gave him a long hard look. Rory held the man's gaze as long as he could and pushed away the fleeting thought that this might turn him into one of the hotel's gargoyles.

"Perhaps we should move on," said Granville Grimm at last. "In fact, I think it would make sense for you to see around a bit, to get an idea of what we have here that might appeal to people."

Rory tensed up. He really did not want to go any further into the building at all. The words "death" and "trap" lodged in his head. At the same time it felt like he was at the point of no return. What would happen to him now if he turned around and said that he wasn't really qualified for the job of rebranding Hotel Grimm?

"Our butler, Grog, will show you around," Granville Grimm gestured with a weary wave of his hand.

There was a squawk from the other side of the room as the man who had opened the front door to Rory, reacted with shock to the fact that he was being expected to do something constructive.

Rory felt equally unenthusiastic about the prospect of a tour with Grog, but kept his feelings to himself. Perhaps it was the grumpy little man who turned guests into statistics for the morgue, thought Rory. Having had his first taste of the inside of the building, Grog's company didn't exactly feel like a guarantee of safety.

"One final thing." Granville Grimm's voice had become sterner. Rory was in no doubt that whatever was about to follow was a command that he was expected to listen to and obey. "Corridor Five is off limits because ..." he paused. "Well, it's just off limits."

Something made Rory want to ask more questions, but it was clear that this part of the conversation was now firmly closed and it quickly followed that the meeting had ended too as Granville Grimm concluded the business. "I look forward to seeing you back here in one week's time with your proposals." With that, he stood up, turned and disappeared into the shadows. Only the click of a door told Rory that Granville Grimm had left the room.

Still in the giant seat, Rory wondered what he was supposed to do next. The grating rasp of Grog clearing his throat, brought him to his senses. His tour was about to start.

10. The guided tour

Rory wondered if Granville Grimm was expecting Grog to provide a tour commentary as they went through the dingy corridors. If that was the case, then the odd little man was falling well short of the mark.

"Ridiculous, utterly ridiculous … don't want more guests anyway … better off without them."

Given this succession of complaints, Rory tried to make out what might be Hotel Grimm's features of interest. However, he found it difficult to pick out many details in the darkness other than a continuation of shabby carpets and raggedy curtains. Nothing in Grog's manner invited any questions, so Rory remained mystified as to what might draw visitors to the hotel. However, as they turned into a corridor to find the walls covered in unframed painted canvases, curiosity got the better of him.

"Who painted these?" Rory called ahead.

"Stop dawdling!" snapped Grog.

Rory slowed down as much as he could without losing track of Grog, sensing something familiar about the paintings. The canvases were clustered around one door on which "GG" was painted in large letters. Granville Grimm himself appeared to be the artist. It occurred to Rory that the fact that the hotel owner was quietly spoken, polite and painted portraits had never appeared in the stories about him.

Grog had already rounded the next corner like an unstoppable, limping toy. Glancing back as he moved on, Rory could have sworn that there was a movement in the shadows. He caught up with Grog wheezing heavily as he eased himself down a short flight of stairs to open some double glass doors.

"What's this?" asked Rory walking into a large space. It had little to offer other than stacks of chairs and a wooden floor badly in need of a sweep.

"Ballroom," snapped Grog.

The room was far less gloomy than everywhere else and looking up Rory realized that it had a glass roof. Hints of the hotel's turrets were visible through a coating of moss and grime. Rory struggled to imagine this drab room full of dancers with a band in full swing.

"Has this been used much in the past?" Rory asked trying to prompt more from his guide. Grog grunted. Frustrated by the continuing lack of information, Rory snapped.

"Do you like dancing yourself?"

Expecting at least a "harrumph" in reply to such an impertinent question, Rory was stopped in his tracks as the butler's whispery voice answered: "I used to." Too taken aback to ask any more, Rory was suddenly distracted by something under his foot.

"What's this?" said Rory looking at the small brass plaque screwed into the floor. The inscription was letters and numbers. "LG: 5.12.29–28.8.48".

Grog looked at Rory long and hard as if trying to work out what to do with him. "You need to look into your local history a little more," he croaked, and with that he turned again and walked towards the door.

That was almost a helpful answer, Rory thought smiling.

Re-entering the labyrinthine hotel, Rory noticed that periodically they passed numbers on the wall as they were about to turn into each corridor. They had already passed two, three and four and moments later Rory looked up and saw a number five.

"Not that way," said Grog seeing Rory pause.

"Is that Corridor Five?" asked Rory, remembering Granville Grimm's comment. "Why is it off limits?"

"It just is," said Grog unhelpfully.

Rory took another step in the direction of the corridor and at that moment the most fearsome noise started; a clattering, banging, wheezing, dreadful sound. Rory yelped and leapt towards Grog.

The butler looked uncomfortable with the noise itself, not to mention the fact that Rory had heard it. He limped away hastily without another word.

"How long has it er ... been like *that?*" asked Rory, now keen to keep close to Grog as some residual crashes and bangs finally dwindled to silence.

"Long enough," Grog replied.

Rory wasn't sure what exactly was going on in Corridor Five, but it sounded a lot worse than a case of dodgy plumbing. Bella Valentine's account of her terrifying time at the hotel popped into his head. He suspected that he had just heard something of whatever it was that she had encountered that had left her with shredded nerves and a slot in *The Chronicle.*

Desperately trying to be positive that the hotel might still reveal some selling points, Rory hit upon an idea. "Is there anywhere that I can see the view from?"

Distinctly unimpressed at this enquiry the wheezing Grog gave Rory a withering look, but grudgingly pointed a gnarled finger towards a small archway. Leaving the butler to recover his breath, Rory began to feel his way up a long spiral staircase. Shoving on a door at the top, he found himself blinking in the daylight, blasted by fresh air. He stepped out onto a tiny balcony perched on one of the hotel's turrets.

Rory looked down, glad that he didn't suffer from vertigo and traced the route he had taken up Scrab Hill. The ledge where he had stopped was one of the hill's clearest features, the cable car station nestled like a little garage just above it. The ledge itself looked like a space large and flat enough to stage a football match, and from this new vantage point, Rory could see that the derelict building, which he had noticed earlier, blended into the hillside at the far end.

Given all that he had seen, Rory wished he could just abseil down the hotel walls in a bid for freedom, but with escape not an option he took a last deep breath of fresh air and ducked back inside and downstairs. Still with the view of the ledge in his mind, Rory remembered his encounter with Ramsay earlier on.

"Would it be possible to see the kitchens?" he asked Grog. Grumbling, the little man turned on his heel and the gloomy tour resumed. After a few twists and turns Rory was surprised to find a bright light shining through a small window in a door ahead. In contrast to everything seen so far at Hotel Grimm, whatever was beyond this door was gleaming. Not only that, but Rory breathed deeply as he realized that an aroma of fried onions and garlic had cut through the smell of damp which had followed them thus far.

Grog opened the door without a hint of creaking hinge. The shine off the smooth surfaces, the bright lights overhead, and the gleaming white and brushed steel of appliances gave the impression that they had just entered a spaceship. The contrast was so great that Rory glanced back, double checking that this room and the twilight world, which the rest of the hotel occupied, really belonged to the same building.

Grog coughed more loudly than usual by way of introduction and a head appeared above some shiny plastic containers on the far side of a central worktop. Ramsay Sandilands' face broke into a thin grin and he waved a hand grandly in welcome.

"Ah you have made it here, my dear boy. Welcome to my world!"

Ramsay looked remarkably different from Rory's earlier encounter with him. He now sported a chef's hat, a white top and, as he moved from behind the worktop, he revealed a pair of pressed black and white-checked trousers. There was no sign of the voluminous hairy coat or matching hat he had been wearing earlier on. Rory's eyes flickered over Ramsay. There was no hint of a twitching pink nose or flickering whisker.

The bewilderment on Rory's face must have been plain to see.

"Surprised again, Rory McKenna?" said the chef, observing his reaction.

"This is just so ... different from everything else I've seen so far," he replied.

"We have standards to keep up here," said Ramsay with an air of self-satisfaction.

"It's amazing," said Rory, "but surely it's hardly being used at the moment?"

"Ah, but what's important," said Ramsay, "is that it's primed and ready to go. As soon as the hotel is back on the map for the right reasons, this kitchen will spring into action."

Rory gave a sceptical look, prompting Ramsay to continue. "I know that day will come. Mark my words. It's just a matter of time." He gave one of his curious rat-like grins and Rory wondered why the man seemed utterly convinced that times were going to change.

A throat-clearing rasp from Grog interrupted them.

"Excuse me!" said Ramsay appalled at the sound and waving them out of his kitchen. Rory stifled a smile as he followed Grog into darkness once more and on to whatever the hotel would offer next.

As with the kitchen, the smell of the next room hit him before the door was opened. This time it was decades of dust created by slowly decaying books that assaulted his nose. Sure enough, stepping through the door he found that the walls of the circular room were lined with books from floor to ceiling. Rails at the top and bottom of the bookshelves allowed a ladder to be pushed around the walls in order to access the highest books.

"Great library," said Rory thinking how much a book lover like Bonnie O'Donnell would love to browse through the contents of this room. Then, remembering Bella Valentine's description of supernatural forces shifting books around, Rory blurted out, "Is this where the poltergeist lives?"

Grog's answer was no more than a strangled noise and a mutter that sounded like "that wretched woman" as he shuffled over to one of two tiny wood-panelled doors which broke the line of the bookshelves. "Right," he said gruffly, twisting the handle. "That's enough. Time to end this."

Rory gulped, imagining Grog bundling him into a cupboard never to be found again. But the butler ducked, went through the door and disappeared from view. Rory hesitated but convinced himself that Grog was taking him to the closing stages of the tour. Taking a deep breath, he entered the tiny staircase. Sure enough, after struggling down a couple of flights of stairs, they emerged from another small door into the hallway where Rory had entered the hotel.

"Good shortcut," said Rory. "And ... um ... thanks for the tour ... I guess I'll head off now... and think a bit about it all. There are obviously a few ... er ... issues to address, so, it's going to be quite a challenge."

Grog looked blankly at him and began to open the front door. Rory realized that this was his last chance to try to get any information.

"Can I ask ... why's the hotel in the state it's in?" asked Rory.

Grog paused. In fact he stopped for so long it was as if someone had switched him off in the act of opening the door. Eventually he spoke, his voice sounding a little strained.

"Since m'lady died."

Rory wasn't sure what to say next, and any other questions he had dried up before he could get them out, leaving him none the wiser about who had died, or when and why this might have made such a big impact.

Stepping over the threshold, it struck Rory that he had managed what others before him had not. He had come to Hotel Grimm and walked out again in one piece.

Knock knock
Who's there?
Guest
Guest who?
Guest who will be the next person to die at
Hotel Grimm …

Joke

11. Clues in the graveyard

As the door thudded closed behind him, Rory was met by a chorus of cawing laughter. Crows circled above him, screeching and cackling.

Rory stumbled away from the hotel, ducking from the noisy black birds as if under an onslaught of sniping comments from Gordon and Gracie Goodman. He ran past the enormous discarded stone wolf, anxious to put some distance between himself and Hotel Grimm and clear his head. One definite souvenir of the visit was that his left shoe was decidedly sticky from whatever he had stood in just after he had crossed the threshold.

Rory was in such a daze, and so intent on getting downhill and back home as quickly as he could, that he didn't notice the path splitting. In less than a minute bushes closed in on him and his backpack snagged on a branch. Startled, Rory looked round. This was not the way that he knew and he realized with a shiver where his wrong turning had taken him. The iron railings and a clutter of headstones showed that he had stumbled across Hotel Grimm's very own graveyard. Surrounded by rocks and bushes, the little rectangular plot was situated on the only level patch of ground on this part of the hill. Feeling very alone and about to head back the way that he had come in double quick time, Rory paused as something caught his eye inside the small enclosure.

He edged closer to investigate a splash of colour that seemed so out of place. His skin tingled as he stepped warily past a bramble patch and through a gap in the railings. *Bad enough visiting Hotel Grimm but wandering through a graveyard too?* thought Rory. *I must be mad.*

But as he forced himself to look, he could see that the little graveyard was a less scary prospect than he had first thought. In fact, fresh flowers placed at the foot of one gravestone, provided the colour that had attracted him. The stone seemed to be a relatively recent addition; its new and polished surface very different from the others, which were weather-beaten and moss-covered. The inscription was clear and simple:

Gwendolen Grimm
Loving wife and mother.
Left us too soon. Sorely missed.

Rory was taken aback. Who was Gwendolen Grimm? Whose wife was she and if she was a mother, then who was her child … or children?

Rory glanced around, curious now about what else the graveyard might have to offer. There was another relatively new-looking memorial stone close by. There was no inscription other than a list of names and the words "In Remembrance." Rory recognised the list as all of the names from the "Too Many Dead Guests" article that he had seen in *The Chronicle* archive … with one big difference — an extra name. "Lottie Gilchrist" appeared at the top of the list. Was there another death that

The Chronicle didn't know about? Who was Lottie Gilchrist? Rory's own list of questions about Hotel Grimm was growing longer the more time he spent there.

Rory soon found that the other stones were for past members of the Grimm family dating back over many decades. The most ornate stone was reserved for Sir Gregory Grimm, whose death was described as a loss to the style and society of the twentieth century and who, it claimed, was responsible for establishing the hotel and creating a classic building of the era.

Realizing that some of the facts in front of him might provide important background, Rory scribbled down a few names and dates in his notebook. Then with a last look round he returned to where he had taken his wrong turning.

About to head downhill, the most amazing smell of home baking spread through the air. As he reached the rock ledge he glanced over at the spot from where he had admired the view earlier on. A small basket covered with a red-checked tea cloth sat in the space. Looking around, but seeing no one, Rory edged closer, and as he drew near noticed that there was a piece of paper pinned to it.

Trust your meeting went well. Compliments of the chef.

RS

Peeking below the cloth, Rory found a selection of still warm scones, pancakes and flapjacks. As a flapjack melted in his mouth, he stopped mid-chew. Just how close had Ramsay Sandilands' rats been to any baking activities? Rory looked suspiciously at the rest of the cakes in the basket. There was no visible sign that any rodents had been too close during the baking process.

However, the thought of Ramsay brought Rory back down to earth with a bump. It was all very well sitting eating cakes and looking at a nice view but that didn't change anything about the shambolic interior of Hotel Grimm and the fact that he was expected to come up with bright ideas in just a week to make it appealing to people. His inadvertent trip to the graveyard reminded him that some of the hotel's more recent guests had ended up with their names on a nearby memorial and that this was a rather large obstacle to overcome.

With a sigh, Rory headed back towards Aberfintry intent on a more productive trip to Boglehole Road in an attempt to tackle the impossible task of Rebranding Hotel Grimm.

12. Back down to earth

"It's been a while Rory. I thought you were ignoring me," said Grandad as Rory entered the front room.

"Now why would I do that?" countered Rory. "Anyway I left you a note the other day. It was you that ignored me!"

"Och, you're just the same as everyone else. Nobody really cares about an old man," said Grandad with a pained expression and the hint of a smile.

"Stick the kettle on son would you?"

Rory checked and found there was enough water in the kettle near to his Grandad's armchair and flicked it on, before slumping down in the seat opposite and sighing deeply.

"That's a big one," said Grandad.

"Was it? I didn't even realize I'd done it," said Rory.

"Something in you wanting to come out?" asked Grandad. Rory said nothing, partly wanting to say what he had really come here to talk about, but also annoyed that his troubled thoughts had been so easily spotted.

"Well, I've a few things on my mind at the moment," said Rory.

"Very mysterious. Anything you need to tell your Grandad about?" Rory didn't reply, allowing the kettle to begin to roar, before putting a steaming mug of tea on the table beside him.

"Help me up a bit, would you?" said Grandad grimacing. Rory heaved under his shoulder to help him get more comfortable. "Don't get old, Rory, just don't get old!" Grandad was always saying it like some sort of joke but seeming to mean it at the same time. Rory never quite knew how to reply.

He sat back in his chair again, but this time it wasn't a sigh that came out. "I was up at Hotel Grimm yesterday," he blurted, surprising himself with the statement.

"I wondered when you were going to mention that," said Grandad.

Rory stopped with his mug halfway to his mouth. "What do you mean?"

Grandad nodded to the telescope which stood on a stand at the window. "I was plotting your progress."

"But, Grandad, you can't see," said Rory with a glance at the magnifying glass he now used for reading.

"Kick a wounded animal, why don't you?" said Grandad.

"I don't mean that nastily but ... well you can't, can you?" he said with a nod towards the white stick that his Grandad refused to use.

"I borrowed someone else's eyes," said Grandad, the lines on his face revealing a mischievous grin.

"Borrowed someone's eyes? Who helped you? And anyway how did you know to look in the first place?" snapped Rory, rattling off the questions.

"You seem surprised to find your old Grandad a step or two ahead of you," said old man giving little away.

"Someone must have tipped you off that I was going ... but I don't understand; no one knew." Rory paused casting his mind around people in the town that he had spoken to in the last few days and then remembered. "Did Malky Mackay come to see you?"

"PC Mackay to you, son. Aye, he did. He said he wasn't too concerned but he thought it best to keep an eye on things. He came here for a bit and watched you get up to the ledge and then you disappeared out of sight. According to him, you were back about two hours later without the spring in your step that there normally is."

At that, it all spilled out as Rory explained everything that had happened from the delivery of the letter right up to his trip to the library and his wrong turning into the graveyard.

"So that's it, Grandad," said Rory at the end of it all. "Rebranding Hotel Grimm. What am I supposed to do?"

"Aye well, it certainly sounds like an interesting piece of work," said Grandad.

"Interesting?" said Rory. "Interesting? Grandad, there are about a thousand better words to describe it ... most of them related to doom and disaster."

"Well, all you can do, is the best you can do, son," said Grandad.

"It's all very well to say things like that, but what if that isn't good enough for Hotel Grimm? Look at what happened to Willie Docherty and Scott MacAndrew."

"Ach don't fuss yourself about that pair of jokers. That's just a bit of typical *Chronicle* nonsense. Anything for a story. You don't believe that, do you? Just because Scott MacAndrew can't pack his van properly he blames Hotel Grimm, and I wouldn't get Willie Docherty to wire a plug for me. The guy's about as useful as a chocolate teapot."

Rory went quiet. He wanted to believe his Grandad but wasn't totally convinced at his attempts to play the situation down.

"Anyway," said Grandad. "I want to hear all about the place. It's been so long since I worked up there. I'm keen to hear what it's like these days."

Grandad said it so casually that his comment almost slipped past Rory before he'd spotted it.

"Worked there?" spluttered Rory, spilling tea down his front as he sat up too quickly.

"Aye son, I worked there for eighteen months. It was years ago mind," said Grandad in a matter of fact tone.

Rory was momentarily stunned. "When? Where? Doing what?" he stammered.

"I was a young apprentice helping out on some building work there," said Grandad shifting in his seat and wincing again as he did so.

"I thought you were a gardener," said Rory. "You worked in the park all your life, didn't you?"

"Aye, I did after that," said Grandad. "At that time, I wasn't long out of school and the owner was ploughing money into the place. He was wanting all sorts of bits and pieces up there so he needed a whole team of builders, joiners and stonemasons. Loads of the lads from school went straight into working up there. The guy had more money than sense really. Statues, gargoyles, stone carvings … complicated pieces of work all over the hotel."

"What did you do?"

"Och, all sorts of stuff. I started off just fetching and carrying, but then I did some stone carving. Did you see the head above the front door? I did some of the work on that."

"Oh, thanks for that," said Rory, remembering the stone face that had greeted him. "That was a lovely welcome, having that thing smirking down at me."

"It was a good piece of work, you cheeky wee thing," said Grandad.

"You must know about other stuff too then," said Rory. "That big stone wolf, for example. And what's the Curse of the Stonemason?"

"Ach, that Curse business. You don't want to trouble yourself with that," said Grandad with a dismissive tone. "That big wolf was made to stand in the hall to greet visitors. What a thought, eh? I should maybe have one here!" he said nodding towards his front door.

"But how could I not have known that you worked up there, Grandad?" said Rory, unable to believe that one of the sources for his background research on Hotel Grimm was in his own family.

"Ach well, you know now," said Grandad taking another glug of tea. "It's been a long time since I was up there."

"What was it like in those days?" asked Rory settling down again after the surprise of Grandad's revelations.

"Well a bit different from what it's like now, I imagine. I think it's gone downhill a bit by all accounts," said Grandad.

"You could say that," said Rory.

"In those days it was a right classy place. It was like a palace inside."

"Who was the owner then?"

"Gregory Grimm. *Sir* Gregory Grimm I should say. He was the reason the place was classy. Slicked back hair and a green velvet smoking jacket with a matching cravate. Dead posh but nice with it. Met a sticky end unfortunately. One of the gargoyles was loosened in a storm and it squashed him flat as he set off for a walk one day. Nasty. Poor man deserved better. He would swan about chatting to us as we worked. Loaded with money so he was."

"Was there money in the family? How come he was so rich?" asked Rory.

"A bit of both. Obviously they were a rich bunch to have that place built to begin with the century before, but Sir Gregory had made his money from tobacco and designing fancy cigarette holders. Smoking was quite the thing then you know. Not like now. It would need some help from a marketing genius to sell *that* as a healthy option these days. Fancy a wee challenge?" Grandad winked at Rory. "Unless you're busy with other work?"

"Grandad, it's not funny. What am I going to do?" said Rory in despair. "I'm supposed to be back there in a week with a plan of what they should do. You know what happens to people who spend any time up at that place. I just want to disappear. Come to think of it they could probably arrange that for me."

"Well ... I'll help you as best I can but isn't there

anyone else that could lend a hand? It's not a job you should have to do on your own."

Rory shrugged, slumping in his seat.

"Your mum and dad?" asked Grandad. Rory gave him a look that said "are you serious?"

"Well, I had to ask," said Grandad.

"You know as well as I do, Grandad," said Rory. "Your daughter lives on Planet Disconnected-from-Reality these days. As for Dad, he *is* connected to reality but never emerges long enough to be any use."

"Aye, aye, fair point," said Grandad with a sigh. "Well....what about your Zizz man. Mr Fankle, was it?"

"Finkleman?" said Rory.

"That's him," said Grandad. "He understands a thing or two about how to sell a product."

"Yeah ... you're right," said Rory. "I could at least drop him an email for some ideas. I suppose I was hoping there was someone a bit closer to home."

"Well what about that lassie at the library? Bonnie?" said Grandad. "She sounds interested and seems a bit of a bright button. What about getting her involved?"

Rory knew that deep down he had wanted to tell Bonnie what he was doing when she approached him the other day. After talking things through a bit more, Rory was also reminded that his Grandad had rarely been wrong about things in the past. By the time he had left Boglehole Road, Rory had resolved that since disappearing was not an option, he would speak to Bonnie at the first opportunity.

13. The masked ball

It took some tossing and turning overnight and a few false starts the next day at school before Rory managed to work up the confidence to approach Bonnie.

"Thanks for these. They were great," he said, holding out the box with the binoculars back inside. "It was really good of you to drop them off for me."

"I thought they'd be handy but I could see you didn't want to talk about it," said Bonnie. "I would ask how it went," she continued, "but I'm not sure that you want me to."

Rory shrugged. "No, I don't mind."

Bonnie's eyes widened at the opportunity. She pulled herself straight in her wheelchair and clapped her hands in glee. "So? Why were you up there? What's going on? Come on, tell me all. Spill the beans. Was it what you expected? I've been dying to ask you. Did you only just get back alive? Have you any scars?"

"Maybe I do mind if that's how you normally ask questions," said Rory managing to get a word in eventually.

"Sorry, sorry," said Bonnie. "It's just that I've never met anyone who's been there."

"You should meet my Grandad," said Rory. "He confessed to me yesterday that he half-built the place."

"Wow! I'd love to meet him," said Bonnie.

"Well, actually I er ... need a bit of help with what Granville Grimm has asked me to do and I'm going to be doing it at my Grandad's. If you came we could kill two birds with one stone."

"Granville Grimm has asked you to do something?" Bonnie squealed.

"SSSSHHHH!" said Rory. "Could you keep it down a bit, please. It's not something I was planning to broadcast."

"Sorry," said Bonnie, speaking in hushed tones and looking furtive. "What's he asked you to do? Is it a marketing job? How exciting!"

"You can have this job if you want," said Rory, "You sound more into it than me." He was wishing again that his encounter with Finkleman all those months ago had never happened. He had emailed the big American about his impossible challenge, trying to describe Hotel Grimm as diplomatically as he could, but had heard nothing back yet.

At least Bonnie was right in front of him and showing an interest so Rory gave her as much of a run through of what had happened as he could before the bell rang to go back inside. As it did, he fixed a time for Bonnie to join him at his Grandad's the next day.

"It's a pleasure to meet you, Bonnie," said Grandad. He was on his feet holding on to the back of his armchair. "I've tidied up a bit as Rory had said you were in the wheelchair. Hope I've given you enough room there," he said jabbing the coffee table with his walking stick. Rory cringed a bit as it seemed as though his Grandad was drawing attention to the fact that Bonnie was in a wheelchair. Bonnie didn't bat an eyelid and was upfront as ever.

"That's fine, Mr Munro. As long as I can get through the door I can usually muddle through. The fact that you've got a ramp up to your front door is the winner for me. Otherwise you and Rory would have been fighting over who got to carry me in."

"You should hear him complaining about that ramp," said Rory. "Might as well hang a banner up saying 'I'm about to keel over,'" he said doing a very good imitation of his Grandad's accent. Grandad grimaced at him.

"I just see these things as a way of getting from A to B," said Bonnie.

"Here," said Grandad, wanting to change the subject. He manoeuvred around his armchair, reaching for the padlocked box. "This is what keeps Rory entertained when he comes here."

"What is it?" asked Bonnie resting the box on her lap and peering at it.

"Just a load of old junk, some people might say. But everything seems to have a story attached to it, so it's all been worth hanging on to."

"Have a go," said Rory. "Grandad's right. It's amazing what's in there."

Bonnie unclasped the padlock and looked inside. Then reaching in as if it was a lucky dip, she rummaged right to the bottom until she pulled out a crumpled and grubby white card, its gold edge nearly rubbed off with age.

"Okay, what's this then?" she asked.

"I don't know," said Grandad glancing over and

looking a bit vague, as he concentrated on getting to his seat. "Some old invitation I think. Try something else."

"That's not like you, Grandad," said Rory. "I thought everything in there had its own story."

Bonnie began to read aloud: *"Sir Gregory Grimm cordially invites you to the Masked Ball at Hotel Grimm on 28th August, 1948."*

"Did you go to that?" asked Rory staring at his Grandad.

"Well, it would have been rude not to," said his Grandad.

"That's not what I mean," said Rory sharply. "I told you I was in the ballroom the other day, but you never mentioned this."

"Calm down son," his Grandad snipped back.

Rory was perplexed. "What else is hidden in there about Hotel Grimm that I should know about?" he asked despairingly, looking over at Bonnie with the box on her lap.

"Nothing's hidden Rory. It's all there waiting to come out," said his Grandad.

"So what was this event like?" said Rory looking at the antique invitation that Bonnie had passed over to him. "Looks very grand."

"All the men who had worked on the building were invited. It was a sort of celebration to mark the end of the work."

"Like a big party then?"

"Aye, well that was the idea, son," said Grandad. Rory noticed that he sounded as though he would much prefer if Bonnie would pull something else out of the box.

"You don't sound too sure about it, Grandad," said Rory. "Was it a party or wasn't it?"

"Well there was a big spread of food, music filling the ballroom, chandeliers sparkling and everyone dressed up to the nines ... so aye, it was a party."

Rory couldn't quite work out what was wrong. Grandad's tone seemed strangely flat. He didn't seem to want to reminisce about what must surely have been Aberfintry's event of the year back in 1948.

"Wait a minute," said Rory. "That's the same year that *The Chronicle* was saying was the turning point for the hotel, and the same year that was on the plaque in the ballroom that I told you about. In fact it might even be the same date. 28th August?"

Rory rooted around in his backpack and pulled out his notebook. Flicking through the pages he came to a note he had made back in the ballroom. "LG:5.12.29– 28.8.48. I knew it." He flicked to the next page. "And then the name "Lottie Gilchrist" was on the memorial in the graveyard. Grandad?"

Grandad was silent. He had a pained expression that Rory could tell wasn't the result of his usual aches and pains.

"Aye well that year and that event was the start of a lot of trouble, that's true enough. But it's not a nice story."

"Grandad, you know I need any information that might lead a way out of this mess. I don't care what kind of story it is if it helps me," Rory said in exasperation.

Grandad cleared his throat. “Well don’t say I didn’t warn you.”

Rory and Bonnie glanced at each other and traded apprehensive looks as Grandad began to speak. “Well, there was this masked ball as you know. The band was in full swing and the dancers were spinning round. While all this was happening, one of the stonemasons had taken his girlfriend outside and up to one of the walkways on the roof to see some of the gargoyles that he’d been working on.”

An uneasy feeling began to creep into Rory as Grandad continued with the story.

“It’s not clear what happened next, but … well … there was … there was a horrible accident.” There was a long pause from Grandad.

“Go on,” said Rory, although deep down he was becoming less sure that he did want to learn more of Grimm’s secrets.

“The girl …” Grandad paused again. He swallowed as if his mouth had gone dry. “The girl lost her footing.”

“From the roof of the hotel?” said Rory.

“Aye, but what made it worse was she sort of … stepped backwards through a glass roof and came crashing into the middle of the dance floor.”

Rory clearly pictured the scene as he had recently been in the ballroom.

“So that was Lottie Gilchrist? Did she …?” asked Rory, not able to finish his sentence.

“Aye. She died then and there. That was about the only mercy. She wouldn’t have known much about it.”

"You're right. That is a horrible story," said Bonnie.

"Sorry," said Grandad looking over at Bonnie. Bonnie shook her head as if to show it wasn't a problem for her. Grandad continued.

"That was the start of people giving the place a reputation. It never got better from that point on. The girl's family tried to get the place shut down. Then there were claims that the girl who died had started to haunt the place. All sorts of nonsense started after that."

"But it's not just nonsense, Grandad, is it?" said Rory. "Other people *have* died too, not to mention the near misses of fires, rockfalls, avalanches and all sorts."

"Aye, well you could choose to look at it that way and some folk do. All I can say is that the Grimms always treated us well when we were working there, but once the first of these things happened, you couldn't raise your voice and say that you thought they were decent people. You were shouted down and folk in the town started to treat you in the same way as they did with them."

The room fell silent. Rory felt a bit uncomfortable that the mood had turned as dark as this. He also realized that although this story probably counted towards his background research, it didn't leave him any further forward for the task he had to do.

"Well, thanks for that cheery little number," he said trying to lighten the atmosphere. "I hate to spoil the fun we're all having here, but we are here to talk about rebranding Hotel Grimm if you remember."

Bonnie smiled, and looked relieved that the silence had been broken. "Oh, terribly sorry, Rory. I'd forgotten that today was all about you."

"It's ever since he won that award," said Grandad pretending to speak quietly to Bonnie behind his hand. "His head has doubled in size you know. I had to get the door widened."

"Well you did me a favour there," said Bonnie as she and Grandad sniggered together.

Rory ignored the jibe. "When you two are quite finished, perhaps we could get on? You both know what I've been asked to do."

"Aye, son, and your first meeting sounded quite eventful."

"I was certainly glad to see you get back safe and sound," added Bonnie.

"Aw thanks," said Rory. "I'm touched by your concern."

"It had nothing to do with you, Rory," said Bonnie with a grin. "I just wanted my binoculars back."

Grandad choked laughing on a mouthful of tea.

Rory was getting impatient. "Come on, guys. Help me here. I *have* to get my head round why *anyone* would want to go to Hotel Grimm and stay there ... and come up with some sensible idea by this weekend."

"Sorry, son, sorry. You're right. We need to give this some serious thought." Grandad pushed himself up in his armchair. "Come on Bonnie, we need to help the lad out here. I think it's fair to say he's a wee tad anxious about all of this."

"Well who wouldn't be!" snapped Rory. "I don't know what's going to happen to me if I don't come up with some ideas."

"Well let's think it through logically," said Bonnie. "Why do people go away from home to stay in other places anyway? And where else do they go? Does Hotel Grimm have any competition?"

"People go away because they want to relax and stay somewhere nice. They want to be looked after. Not go to a complete dive like that place," grumbled Rory. "Sit back and take the weight off your feet while having some giant moths flap round your head … oh, and by the way, there's a chance you'll never leave. It's a really strong set of selling points, isn't it?"

"People go away to see somewhere new," said Grandad. "That's what I miss these days."

"Yeah. Holidays are all about getting away from what you normally do, and seeing something completely different," said Bonnie.

"Like what?" said Rory.

"Well, sightseeing, like going to a new part of the country. Or even to some special place like a museum or a country house … or a zoo. You know … people love seeing how others live, or seeing curious animals and all their funny little habits."

"Aye you're right, Bonnie," Grandad chipped in. "The other thing is that people these days are all into their leisure sports are they not? They weren't when I was young."

"Oh, here we go," said Rory. "Stand by for a lecture about the good old days."

"Hang on a minute, it's true," said Grandad. "Folk now are off skateboarding, mountain biking, rock climbing, that bungy jumping thing, scuba diving … goodness knows what else. There was none of that in my day. Who knows what'll be next? People seem to want to escape and get their adrenaline rush at the weekend and then return to normal life on a Monday."

"That's why people go to amusement parks too," said Bonnie. "People love the big rides to get a bit of a thrill … a bit of escapism."

"If people want excitement, then Hotel Grimm might be able to offer them something," said Rory mulling it all over. "There's an element of excitement there if something awful has happened to each of the last few guests."

"That's not exciting, that's just horrible! That's not the route to go down at all!" said Bonnie.

"No, no, I think it is … I think that's it!" said Rory dropping his notebook and clapping his hands. "That's it! Excitement, getting away from it all, a glimpse at a different world … all of those things. That's it!"

"What do you mean *that's it?*" said Grandad looking confused. "What's what? I can't keep up here."

"Well, it's obvious. Why didn't I think of this before? Those things are what set Hotel Grimm apart from any other hotel. You get a chance to look into a different world. There are curious people with bizarre behaviour for you to see. Go to a place where you'll really feel like you've escaped from everyday life. Where else can you feel your way around in the dark and not know what you've stepped in? Not only that but you can have the ultimate fright ride ... better than any roller-coaster, because you don't know if you'll come out alive!"

Grandad nodded slowly, beginning to get what Rory was suggesting. Bonnie, however, was shaking her head. Rory was oblivious to both, caught up in his own world of ideas.

"I can see the advertising campaign now. "Do you dare to stay at Hotel Grimm? Don't just look at it ... try staying there! See the Grimms in their natural habitat in the ultimate test of survival!"

Rory was on a roll. He could feel relief flooding through him in great waves. It dawned on him that he had actually found a way to solve the impossible problem Granville Grimm had presented him with.

"This is what sets Hotel Grimm apart from anywhere else. The weird butler, the odd owner, the bizarre chef *and* the chance that you might not get out alive. That's their Unique Selling Point!" He beamed in delight and punched the air. All of the gloom of the last few days had lifted from him.

In contrast, Bonnie folded her arms firmly and sat in silence watching Rory congratulate himself.

"Yah beauty! I've cracked it! There *is* an answer!" The normally laid back Rory jumped up on a seat, his arms outstretched. "You are looking at not just the Zizz Boy, you are looking at the world's newest superhero ... *Marketing Man!*"

A noise interrupted Rory's proclamation. It was a slow ironic handclap from Bonnie.

"Thank you, thank you," said Rory not realizing immediately that Bonnie wasn't sharing his enthusiasm.

"Come on! Get a bit more excited than that will you?" he said, now starting to feel a bit silly standing on a chair. "Don't you realize how brilliant this is?"

Bonnie looked away and continued to say nothing, and it was Grandad who spoke first.

"I'm not so sure, son. You've got a point that these things are what set them apart, but that doesn't make it right to highlight them."

"Got a point?" snapped Rory. "You can't possibly disagree. It's so obvious that this has to be the answer. The place is really scary so why not turn that fact into its strong point? Can't you just see it all now? "*Need excitement and challenge in your life? Want the weirdest weekend ever? Come and stay at Hotel Grimm. If you make it through one night you get the second free!*"

"It's not right," said Bonnie quietly.

"Well maybe two nights and you get the third one free," said Rory.

"I don't mean that. The whole idea is just not right."

"What do you mean "not right"? It is *so* right!"

"No Rory, it's *not* right. You can't just bring people in to gawp at Granville Grimm or anyone else like they're some kind of freakshow. You're the one that said he wasn't nearly as scary as you had thought he was supposed to be."

"I know, but with a bit of spin we can build that up a bit," said Rory beginning to enthuse again. "I appreciate what you're saying Bonnie ... but you're wrong on this one."

"Well you are the marketing genius," said Bonnie frostily.

"Do you know," said Rory with new-found confidence, "If I have cracked this one, then I *am* a marketing genius."

Bonnie had one more go at challenging him. "But can't you see what I'm trying to say? For starters it's just rude. Your client is, shall we say, a bit out of the ordinary. Correct me if I'm wrong but your only plan is that people come and stay to see him for that reason. Then you would hope that they would tell their friends how odd he is so that they come too?"

"Umm ... pretty much yeah," said Rory unfazed by Bonnie's question. "And your problem is ...?"

"And in the mean time," said Bonnie, "The fact that people have died is a bonus just to add a bit of spice to the proceedings for you, is it?"

"If that's true, son, then you're just operating at the same level as most people in this town." Grandad looked at him with sadness as Bonnie folded her arms crossly.

"But their weirdness is what they have going for them!" said Rory.

"Is that the best that you can do?" said Bonnie not letting the issue lie. "Picking on the most obvious thing about someone and making fun of it? That's just what goes on in the playground. I mean Gracie and Gordon Goodman would be proud of you. That's the kind of thing they would have come up with."

She was moving her wheelchair backwards and forwards as much as she was able in the tight confines of the room, agitated with the debate.

Rory looked bemused as Bonnie continued. It was her turn to rant. "I mean how would you like it, Rory? Come and stay at Hotel McKenna … marvel at the boy genius. A world expert at the age of eleven. How bizarre! See him in the flesh! We could put you on a pedestal in the hall so that people could ogle at you. How would you feel?"

She hadn't finished. "So, what about me? What's my Unique Selling Point then? What makes me different from other people?" Rory looked uncomfortable and stared at his feet.

"Get lost," he said feeling thoroughly confused and wishing that the conversation would come to an end. Despite Bonnie's strongly held opinions, Rory was still convinced that he had hit on a good idea.

There's a muckle big painting in our town
It makes you smile if you're feeling down
The reason is without a doubt
That Hotel Grimm has been left out

Children's chant

14. The mural and the mystery painter

Rory didn't know if he was coming or going. He thought he had found a new friend and ally to help in his impossible challenge, but no sooner had he sat down to talk with her than he had lost her. He couldn't really see why his ideas had created such a sore point, but the constructive time together at his Grandad's that he had been looking forward to, had finished very frostily indeed. At least he felt reassured that he had come away from there with a plan about how to approach the meeting at Hotel Grimm on Saturday, even if Bonnie and his Grandad had a different opinion. Since then, he had received some support from one quarter at least. Harvey Finkleman had finally returned his e-mail.

> Rory, my apologies for a late and short reply here. Things are a little bit crazy here as Zizz is about to launch in China.
>
> It was good to hear from you. I have been meaning to contact you for a while as I have some curious family business to let you know about. I'll be back in touch about that soon. I wasn't totally clear about the job you are taking on, but it sounds like you wanted my thoughts on "selling the unsellable" as you put it.

> For the record, I would say that I don't believe you can sell everything. There isn't a marketing answer for every product. Some things are unsellable because they are not what people want, so no matter how hard you try you will always come up short.
>
> The important thing to keep in mind is "What do people actually want?" If you have what they want, then it's about finding the best way to sell it!
>
> Apologies for the rush. Am off to Beijing in 3 hours time! Do come back to me if you want any clarification.
>
> H Finkleman

Rory couldn't think what kind of "curious family business" Finkleman could want to let him know about, but more importantly, the American's analysis of the current situation was that Hotel Grimm might well fit the category of "unsellable." It might just not be what people want. If that was true, then Rory faced being in the position of disappointing Granville Grimm, which was not where he wanted to be.

It was three days later that Rory saw Bonnie buzzing over to him at the end of the school day with a determined look on her face. He steeled himself for an onslaught.

"I need you to come with me," she said. "There's something you have to see."

"What?" asked Rory, relieved that the conversation sounded more constructive than he could have predicted.

"I can't really tell you. I just need you to look at something and tell me what you see," said Bonnie turning away.

"Listen," said Rory, wanting to bring up their previous conversation, but having to stride fast to keep up. Her chair was whizzing ahead of him at top speed. Bonnie stopped sharply and Rory piled into the back of her.

"Forget the other day," she interrupted. "We have different opinions on that. This is something else that we need to think about." She buzzed away shouting "Come on!" as she went.

Rory headed after her, without the slightest idea of where they were going. A few minutes later, they were outside the library and Bonnie had stopped at the mural of Aberfintry.

"I don't understand," said Rory stopping beside her. "What am I supposed to be looking at?"

"Have a closer look than if you were just passing by," said Bonnie, looking hard at the mural herself. "Tell me what you see."

Rory stared at the scene, not really sure what it was Bonnie was expecting him to pick out.

"I always come this way to school," she said, "and I can tell you that something is changing each day, or rather during the night. Keep looking and see if you spot anything."

Rory stood and looked long and hard at the mural. It was like one of those "spot the difference" puzzles as he tried to think what it usually looked like and what might be different now. The mural showed Aberfintry, a familiar enough scene with many local landmarks picked out in detail.

Everything seemed in order to Rory and he was on the verge of giving up when he saw it. "What's *that* doing there?" he said in amazement.

"Exactly!" said Bonnie.

"But that's the *one* thing that wasn't supposed to be in this painting!" said Rory shaking his head in disbelief.

Bonnie and Rory stood looking at the mural of the town. Aberfintry was there looking just as it should, but in the background, as if emerging through the mist on top of Scrab Hill, was the outline of Hotel Grimm. The reason that the mural had been created and the one thing that had been deliberately left out, was putting in an appearance all by itself.

"That gives me the creeps," said Rory. "It's like the place itself doesn't like the fact that it's been left out of the picture." He shivered.

Bonnie shook her head firmly. "Snap out of it, Rory! You sound like the front page of *The Chronicle.* Paintings don't just paint themselves. Whoever's behind this is doing a really good job," she continued. "Someone is adding to it ever so subtly each night. It's very clever. They're doing just enough so that people don't notice."

"You did," said Rory.

"I have the distinct advantage of being at the right level," said Bonnie manoeuvring her chair, "...and of being more observant than most," she added with a smile. "The thing is, if anyone else cottons on, especially if *The Chronicle* gets hold of the story then they'll kick up a real stink if they think that somehow the hotel is forcing its way into the mural."

"You're right," said Rory, thinking that even worse publicity might stretch the chances still further of anyone staying at Hotel Grimm. "I can see their headlines now… "Hotel's Hand of Evil Creeps into the Heart of Our Community". We should get to the bottom of this before *The Chronicle* starts putting its own spin on it."

"Hey look it's the Worm!"

Rory and Bonnie jerked around to find Max Fletcher and Marnie di Angelo passing a few yards away.

"Yeah, she's got a new apprentice," said Marnie. "She's teaching Zizz Boy how to read."

"Just don't ask him what his choice of reading material is. He must be sick in the head." Max tapped his head as the two walked on.

"Ignore them," said Bonnie.

"It could have been worse," said Rory. "At least it wasn't the Goodmans."

"They're all the same," said Bonnie. "Identical in fact. They all have only one brain cell each." Rory smiled. "Anyway, forget about them. There's some simple explanation to this. I know there is," said Bonnie as Rory tried to look as closely as he could at the mural without drawing attention.

"It's always a bit different by the time we go to school so there really is only one thing to do," said Bonnie.

"What?" said Rory.

Bonnie looked at him. "Well it's obvious. If something is happening at night then …"

"… we need to be there to see it," said Rory, finishing the sentence for her.

"No, but nearly," said Bonnie. "*You* need to be there to see it."

"Me, why me?" asked Rory.

"Independent I may be, but it would pretty hard for me to sneak out of my house at night without anyone spotting me," said Bonnie. "But from what you've said, getting out of your place should be a breeze."

"So what exactly will your contribution be to this, apart from having the bright idea in the first place?" said Rory, wishing that he had never opened his big mouth about his distracted parents.

"I'll help you plan how to do it and then I'll stay up and text you through the night."

"Mmm," said Rory looking at the dim outline of Hotel Grimm on the mural, trying to convince himself that the turrets and spires didn't have a life of their own, and hadn't changed in the few minutes that they had been standing there. He couldn't quite work out just how he had managed to get himself signed up for this particular task.

Rory was still wondering the same thing eight hours later as he took up position at the foot of Lachlan Stagg's statue. The Zizz campaign and all that it had resulted in, had forced him into situations that he would normally have tried to avoid. Yet here he was, about to spend a night outside, trying not to be seen by anyone and hoping to identify whoever or whatever was discreetly vandalizing the town's pride and joy. This wasn't really his scene at all. Still, Bonnie had been right about one thing. Getting out of his house had been extremely straightforward; a combination of vague, or otherwise engaged, parents, a conveniently located ground-floor bedroom with a smoothly-opening window and some dark clothing ... and here he was.

Admittedly, it wasn't the best hiding place but he could peek round the corner and see the mural easily. The only problem that he had was the difficulty in moving freely as he had five layers of clothes on to ensure he kept warm through the night. The backpack at his feet had been carefully put together by Bonnie, complete with a blanket, snacks and an enormous torch, and he was under instructions to text her every thirty minutes with an update. After three of these updates, Rory had run out of things to put other than "a bit darker. no sign of anything."

He slumped down and decided to feel cold and miserable for a bit and to curse his luck at having to spend the night outside. He was interrupted by a buzzing in his pocket as his phone vibrated. The message from Bonnie was "I bet uve nodded off. Pay attention."

Rory had almost forgotten his reason for being there, when a routine casual glance made his jaw drop. A hunched figure was working away on the giant painting, but Rory hadn't even seen or heard anyone arrive. Fleetingly, he thought of the option of sneaking home back to the comfort of his bed, but he knew that Bonnie would spot differences in the painting the next day and he would be found out. With shaky hands he pulled out his phone and texted, "Its started" as she had instructed. Since the hotel was only emerging a little at a time with a few carefully chosen details, Bonnie and Rory had concluded that whoever was responsible might not be there for very long.

Rory watched closely. Although absorbed in what they were doing, the painter jerked around every few seconds as if checking that he wasn't being watched. Crouched behind the statue, Rory remained undetected even when the phone vibrated in his hand. The little screen lit up in the darkness. Bonnie's text simply said "Its time." Rory hit reply with the message "Here goes." He shivered as he put the phone in his pocket not really feeling ready for a confrontation.

Holding his breath and moving round the corner of the statue with as much stealth and as little sound as he could, Rory stood in position. The painter continued to work away, unaware of what was about to happen. Rory's finger hovered over the switch on Bonnie's enormous torch for a moment then, knowing there was no way back, Rory winced and switched it on. The beam shone straight at the mural and the figure at the wall flinched and froze in the bright light, completely motionless at first, as if he thought he might remain invisible by not moving. Then, Rory thought he saw the person tense, ready to make a run for it. He steeled himself, preparing to give chase if need be, but the moment passed. The painter seemed to think otherwise, the shoulders relaxed, and he turned into the light, shielding his eyes from the glare.

"Who are you?" challenged Rory in as commanding a voice as he could muster.

There was no reply.

"I like what you've painted," said Rory. "It's very clever. I just wanted to see who'd done it."

"So now you can see me," said a young male voice. "Can you switch that light off? I can't see a thing."

"Sorry," said Rory clicking the torch off. As he peered into the darkness he made out a tall thin lad in his mid-teens rubbing his eyes. As the hands moved from his face, Rory saw a sharp nose and angular cheekbones. He looked as though he had grown faster than his body could keep up with.

"I'm Rory McKenna. Who are you?" said Rory edging forwards.

"I know who you are," said the boy, seemingly quite relaxed as he bent to gather some of his painting materials together.

"How come?" said Rory, baffled that the mystery painter was more informed than he was.

"You've been in my house," said the boy.

"When was I at your house? Who are you?" asked a bemused Rory.

There was a long pause as the boy weighed up the situation. A slow smile drifted onto his face, as if amused by Rory's confusion. "I'm Grimson Grimm."

Rory's mind raced. *A boy called Grimm? How could he have missed the fact that there was another living Grimm?*

"You didn't know about me, did you?" said Grimson Grimm looking up from his backpack. "Well you should know that there is more to the Grimm family than what you read."

"So why have you been doing this?" asked Rory pointing at the mural.

Grimson paused, surveying his work. "It seemed a bit ... incomplete. I thought I'd finish it off. So what about you?" continued the boy. "Have you done anything yet?"

Rory looked confused once more. "I mean ... how are you getting on with what my Dad asked you to do?" Grimson stood with arms folded as if planning to go nowhere until he was answered.

It was Rory's turn for a long pause. *What was he supposed to say to that? How was he supposed to describe his progress in rebranding Hotel Grimm?* Suddenly a few things fell into place.

"You were watching when Grog showed me round, weren't you?"

"Sure was. You seemed to have trouble keeping up with him," replied Grimson with a smirk.

"Those paintings in the corridor are yours too, aren't they? The 'GG' on the door isn't for Granville Grimm, it's for you, isn't it?"

"So you *are* quite sharp then. I wasn't sure if the Zizz Boy would be all he was cracked up to be."

The hairs on the back of Rory's neck shot up as he felt the world of Zizz Cola come all too sharply into focus. He was saved by the phone buzzing in his pocket and remembered that Bonnie still had no idea about the identity of the painter.

As he answered, Rory was reminded just how determined a character Bonnie O'Donnell was. Not content with Rory's explanation of who he had just discovered, she demanded to speak to Grimson himself. He in turn looked bemused. Rory was quietly amused and tried not to stare at the one-sided scene of Grimson being interrogated over the phone, having to explain how often he had been coming to paint, how long he had spent on each session and whether anyone up at the hotel knew about what he had been doing. Grimson was finally saved by Rory's phone bleeping to signal that the battery was running low.

"I thought I told you to make sure it was fully charged," snipped Bonnie, as Rory took the phone again.

"I did. You've sapped it of all its energy," said Rory.

"I know the feeling," said Grimson with a grin.

"I heard that," said Bonnie.

"Good," said Rory. "Now go and get some beauty sleep."

"Don't need it," said Bonnie.

Rory switched his phone off before she could say any more.

"Right I'll get the cable car back home," said Grimson straightening up from filling his back-pack.

"It was good to meet you," Rory replied, trying not to react to the fact that Grimson was about to travel by a mode of transport that no Aberfintry resident would think of risking their life in.

"When are you next up at the hotel? You should come and see me," said Grimson.

"The day after tomorrow. Can you put in a good word for me?" asked Rory.

"I tend not to see my Dad that much," said Grimson closing the last of the clips on his back-pack and swinging it onto his shoulder. "I sort of do my own thing."

"I know the feeling," said Rory. "What are you going to do about this?" he said gesturing at the mural.

"Well, I wasn't planning to do much more," said Grimson. "I wanted to make sure the place was there but not too obviously. I think you and Bonnie have proved that I've just about reached that point."

Rory nodded in agreement.

"Right, I'm off home. See you up there soon," Grimson said looking back over his shoulder as he strode away and disappeared into the darkness.

Home? thought Rory. *Hotel Grimm?* If only rebranding were that simple.

15. Make or break

The second trip up Scrab Hill and into Hotel Grimm seemed more straightforward to Rory. From the start he knew that he'd survived one encounter so he felt that he had every chance of making it through another. Secondly, he was armed with his very own solution to the challenge of rebranding Hotel Grimm, a smart folder containing five crisp sheets of typed paper outlining his ideas. Not only that, but another journey there meant that he had the chance once more to enjoy the view of Aberfintry, while in Grandad and Bonnie he had people who knew where he was going, even if they didn't agree with what he was going to say when he got there.

It was also less alarming on a second occasion to have the door opened by a butler who was as disconcerting as Grog was.

"So there you have it," concluded Rory after presenting his suggestions to Granville Grimm, who was seated once again at the far end of the table.

Rory rustled his papers together, feeling happy that he had presented his suggestions enthusiastically and clearly. He had pointed out that the hotel had unwittingly carved out a niche for itself. Recent trends in guests not making it back down the hill, whilst unfortunate, had meant that the hotel could be viewed as a place of excitement and intrigue. The family's reclusive nature and their slightly unusual staff, meant that there was curiosity value for visitors intrigued by the Grimms.

"Think of yourselves as a kind of royal family or a family in a soap opera," he said. "People want to know about you're going to do next."

As he finished there was an awfully long pause. In the gloom, Granville Grimm had put down his copy of the report and pressed his hands together as if he was praying. Rory cleared his throat nervously, not sure whether to make another move and wondered momentarily if praying might be a good activity for himself. He tried to read the reaction on the man's face. The only hint of emotion was a flicker on his brow as if a fly had brushed past. Eventually, the silence was broken by a quiet, calm voice.

"Are these serious suggestions?" asked Granville Grimm.

Rory was so taken aback at this opening line that he had nothing to say in response.

"Is there a problem?" Rory heard his own voice quavering as he asked the question.

"No there is not *a* problem," said Granville Grimm, "There are lots and lots and lots of problems. Correct me if I'm wrong," he continued in his measured, polite voice. "The fact that my family doesn't fit with people's expectations, and that there have been a series of deeply unfortunate accidents, are what you want to make the centre of your campaign? That is both disappointing and insulting."

Rory could feel panic beginning to rise inside. Swallowing hard and pulling at his collar to let off some heat, he tried to play things as cool as he could. "I'm sorry to hear that," he said, as his mind whirled.

"You seem to consider the main attraction to be that we are odd and possibly dangerous," said Granville Grimm.

"I didn't say that," said Rory, knowing that at the very least he had thought it.

"No, you said ..." Granville Grimm flicked back through the report, "unusual ... out of the ordinary ... different. You seem to suggest that the hotel ought to become some kind of zoo and we are to be on display."

"Er ... it's not like that," said Rory thinking that this was nearly how Bonnie had interpreted his idea.

"It sounds like that," said Granville Grimm sliding the report across the table top to Rory as if he had seen quite enough of it and wanted it nowhere near him now.

Rory knew he had to say something but didn't know what to say. "It's just that ... well ... your run of misfortune *is* your Unique Selling Point. There's no other hotel like yours ... anywhere. So that's the thing ... er ... that's the ... er ... strength I thought you should play to."

Granville Grimm continued to observe Rory through his steepled fingers. "We don't want to be set up as some kind of bizarre freakshow," he said. "Everybody is different, aren't they? Why should that mean that people have to make a big issue out of it? I mean you seem a bit peculiar to me. I know of no other eleven-year-old marketing expert but

I'm not planning to send anyone to gawp at you."

Rory was appalled at how closely Granville Grimm's reaction mirrored Bonnie's opinion. He could imagine her beside him, so keyed up she'd be doing 360 degree turns, muttering "I told you so" in his ear. The meeting was rapidly going downhill and Rory realized that he desperately needed to buy himself some time to think, before he slid further towards personal disaster.

"I wonder if I could use your facilities," he said in a moment of inspiration.

"I beg your pardon?" said Granville Grimm.

"I need to go to the toilet," said Rory.

"Ah yes, yes, of course. Top of the stairs on the first floor," said the hotel owner with a dismissive wave.

Rory slipped off his seat and scuttled towards the door, breathing hard and relieved that he had salvaged a few minutes to think, even if it meant being alone in a corridor in Hotel Grimm.

"WAIT," called Granville Grimm. "I see no point in continuing this meeting on your return. Your approach is not what I had hoped for. Not at all. Please return in a week with an alternative. A significantly *different* alternative." With that, Granville Grimm left his chair and melted into the darkness.

Rory felt a strange mixture of relief that the meeting was over already, and lingering dread that he was firmly back at square one. He also felt that he really did now need the toilet.

With his mind still whirling, Rory wasn't really

thinking straight as he headed through the doorway into what he had been told was a bathroom. In the half-light, he edged along the side of the bath and reaching the faint outline of the toilet, raised the lid. Instinctively, he glanced down. It seemed deeper and darker than a normal toilet. His heart racing, Rory was weighing up just how much he needed to go when he detected a movement at the bottom of the toilet bowl.

"Oi! What do you think you are doing?" Grog appeared in the doorway and was even less impressed than usual.

"Er … I needed the toilet," said Rory.

"In HERE? In HERE?" shouted Grog.

"Well it is a bathroom," reasoned Rory.

"Oh no, I don't believe it! My babies … be careful of my babies!" squawked Grog. "Has he harmed you? What has he done?" Grog hobbled further into the room as Rory froze. The thought of what Grog's "babies" might be, sent fear and nausea pulsing through him at the same moment. The room suddenly felt colder, damper and darker and there was no mistaking the occasional wet slithering and slapping noises that his mind could no longer blank out.

His eyes now adjusted to the gloom, Rory forced himself to look down at the toilet. A metre of snake had slid dripping over the lip of the bowl and was easing itself on to the floor by Rory's feet. It looked as though there were a few more metres to follow.

He stepped backwards his heel connecting with a solid object. Wincing as he looked down in trepidation he found a bucket full of white salamanders writhing blindly in a wet slapping ball. Rory lurched to one side and put out a hand to steady himself, knocking a gecko off the wall and sending three others scurrying towards the ceiling.

By now he was spinning around in slow motion trying to put his feet and hands nowhere and somewhere at the same time. Anywhere to avoid contact with whatever the next creature might be. As he did so, Grog hurpled over towards him as fast as his twisted frame allowed.

"No, not there! BE CAREFUL!" shouted Grog, as Rory swayed and spun. "No, not there, that's the newts....oh my poor loves," Grog paused to caress a large toad lazing on the edge of the bath as though to reassure it.

Rory finally staggered to a stop beside a large metal drum near the door. Looking inside he found that it was full of dead mice. Rory whimpered.

Grog spat out an explanation, "Well the big ones have to eat something tasty, don't they, and there's no shortage of the little blighters in this place.

"Bentley, get back in your home," he continued, directing his attention to the snake which had prompted the commotion. It appeared to look lazily at Grog, its tongue flickering in and out then promptly began to reverse back down the toilet.

Rory stumbled out of the bathroom, his heart thudding against his chest. Suddenly the dank corridor seemed as appealing as a cosy teashop compared with Grog's pet sanctuary. He leant against the wall and wiped the sweat from his brow, making a mental note that the rooms next to this bathroom would be particularly difficult to let to guests.

"I heard a commotion and wondered if you were involved," said a familiar voice. Rory looked around to find that Grimson had emerged from the shadows, a mixture of amusement and mild concern mingling in his voice.

"I shall never sit on a toilet again," said Rory.

"Things going well in your rebranding plans then?" asked Grimson with mischief in his eye.

"This job is *not* getting any easier," said Rory, looking back with disbelief at the room he had just come from. "Did I really see that in there?"

"I wouldn't worry about it," said Grimson. "Grog knows what he's doing. He's been looking after those creatures for years. One of them caused a scene *once* when it escaped and ended up in a guest's bedroom, but on the whole they're very well behaved. So is Grog really," he finished with a smile.

"Mmm," said Rory unconvinced and looking around himself to check that no creature had decided to attach itself to him.

"Anyway if you want some light relief why don't you come and see my room."

Rory accepted the offer and walking alongside Grimson through the hotel, he realized that he now had a guide who might actually answer some of his questions. "What's the story with this Corridor no one's supposed to go near? It all sounds a bit mysterious."

"Yeah, that is an odd one," replied the lad. "I'm not one for superstition but even that one gets me. There's something there that gets seriously unhappy if you go anywhere near it. I've stuck a toe in the end of the corridor but that was enough for me. The sound it makes does not encourage you to go any further. It never causes any bother otherwise so we all just leave well alone."

16. The gallery

The smell of paint caught Rory in the back of the nose and throat at the same time as he entered the door marked "GG." At the end of the bed stood an easel and scattered all around its legs were curled up tubes of oil paint, brushes sticking out of pots, a palette and a mound of raggedy, paint-smeared cloths. Apart from a couple of heavy dark wardrobes and chests of drawers the room seemed to be little other than a bedroom and a studio.

The other noticeable feature was that there was little wall space left, which explained why paintings were now being hung outside in the corridor. Every inch was covered in portraits of all shapes and sizes. Rory turned slowly around. From floor to ceiling he was completely surrounded by people, all seeming to look blankly into the room.

"I love faces," said Grimson closely watching Rory's reaction.

"So I see," said Rory.

"Every face is unique," Grimson went on. "I always think that each one tells a story of its own; where it's been, what it thinks of life now, what it hopes for the future. That's what I like trying to capture when I paint someone."

Rory wasn't quite sure that he followed, but as Grimson talked, he walked slowly around the room looking more closely into the eyes of the faces that the boy had painted.

Six portraits were grouped together. None of them were people that he recognised but Rory soon worked out that the combination of four men and two women, and the ages and appearances of the people featured meant that they were the six dead guests.

"Is that not a bit sick?" said Rory nodding towards the collection.

"Quite the opposite," said Grimson. "It seemed like a good memorial — I felt like each of them should be captured for who they were … not just in a sensationalist paragraph in the local paper."

Rory nodded appreciatively, then stopped in his tracks as a familiar face appeared before him.

"That's my Grandad!" he said.

"Oh right," said Grimson, "That one is a few years old now. I really enjoyed doing that one. He looked like a real character. Is it like him?"

Rory thought of the old man slouched in an armchair who seemed to be fading away with every visit. He looked at the portrait. The face staring back appeared warm, wise and with a twinkle in his eye.

"Well, yes it is, but I'd forgotten he looked like that," said Rory.

Rory's attention was taken by another one. He could see someone familiar but couldn't work out who it was. It showed an upright man with a proud gaze and a look of fearlessness. Peering into the eyes Rory realized that if he imagined the person in the painting with a stooping, limping walk, ruffled hair and a hacking cough, then it would turn into Grog.

He turned in confusion to Grimson who spoke up. "That man is full of surprises. He's picked up some injuries over the years and they've not left him in the best of humour, or the best of health. But if he's on your side, you could trust your life to him."

Rory felt sure that Grimson was now stretching things a bit but didn't feel that he could say so. He continued to move around the room taking in more of the portraits. He saw Mrs Trinder-Kerr looking organized and efficient and more friendly than Rory's recent experience at the library suggested, Malky MacKay appearing upright and approachable even just from the painting of his head and shoulders, and then his own mother Momo McKenna, bright-eyed, as if a new idea had just captured her attention. Lots of familiar faces, and each with Grimson's distinctive edge to them.

"How do you manage to do these paintings? It's not as if you've had people posing for you."

"It's a combination of two things. I have a bit of a photographic memory but to kick it off I go in the cable car."

"Do you really risk your life in that thing?" said Rory. "How does that help? Nobody else ever goes in there and it's surely too far away from the town to see anything?"

"Ah, that's where you're wrong," said Grimson. "You should go in sometime and check out the telescopes that Stobo has fitted in there. They are the coolest thing. The detail you get is amazing."

"My Grandad has a telescope. I like using it,"

said Rory trying to be polite and knowing that setting foot in the cable car was not something he intended to do.

Rory scanned the walls to see who else he knew.

"That's Bonnie!"

"Ah, that makes sense," said Grimson. "She definitely seemed a bit of a character on the phone the other night."

Rory looked long and hard. The portrait showed her from the waist up. She looked lively, quirky and bright. In fact, she looked so full of life that she might just start speaking or even step right off the canvas. But Rory felt unsettled. He couldn't work out what was different about her from the Bonnie he knew, but there was definitely something. Something wasn't right. Something was missing.

"The wheelchair ... you've not painted her wheelchair."

"I didn't think I needed to," said Grimson in a matter of fact voice. "I never paint furniture into anyone's portrait."

Before Rory could think it through he came face-to-face with himself. The face looking back at him seemed a bit thinner than he thought he looked and there was something else that took him by surprise.

"I look a little bit worried," he said to Grimson.

"Are you?" replied Grimson.

"Sometimes," said Rory thinking just how worried he had been recently.

"I did it after you were up here the other week," said Grimson. "I was watching you as you went around with Grog."

Rory was relieved to get confirmation that at least some of the shadowy figures, which he had thought he had seen in the background on his tour around the hotel, must have been no more than Grimson the artist eyeing up his next subject.

"Well, I guess it's fair to say that I was pretty worried at that stage. I didn't know if I was going to get out of here alive," he said.

"Well, there you go," said Grimson with an air of being satisfied but unsurprised that another of his paintings had been declared accurate. "You people in the town really are prone to exaggeration, aren't you?" he added.

Rory couldn't think of what to say in response. Here in the relative comfort of Grimson's room, the hotel seemed to have lost its sinister trappings.

"Have you done yourself?" asked Rory.

"Yeah. I'm just over there," said Grimson pointing to the far corner of the room. Rory was curious to see just how Grimson pictured himself, given the accuracy he seemed to have achieved with everyone else. Rory found the picture, a thin face looming out of a dark background. What jumped out at him were Grimson's eyes. They were piercing and intense and seemed to look right at you and into you.

There was just one painting that had two people in it. Rory didn't recognise the woman and at first glance thought that the man was new to him too. The woman was striking with a pale slender face, long dark hair pulled tightly back and a scarlet dress. With a closer look Rory realized with a start that the upright, smiling man with close cropped hair beside her, was a younger, brighter and happier Granville Grimm. Rory wasn't quite sure what to say. The picture was so markedly different from the man downstairs that he wanted to comment but felt embarrassed to make reference to the fact. Rory realized that Grimson's lean, striking looks came from his mother.

"Is that your Mum?" he asked.

"Yeah."

"Was that her gravestone I saw the other day?" Grimson said nothing in response. "I'm sorry she's … sorry she's not here any more," said Rory.

"Me too," said Grimson.

"Your Dad looks kind of different," said Rory. Grimson's responses dried up. "Should I stop saying stuff?" said Rory.

"Sometimes I'm up for talking about it and sometimes I'm not," said Grimson.

"That's okay," said Rory. "It's up to you."

"It's been a few years now. Mum got ill and then just went downhill really. It's been a bit rubbish since she died. That came after all the accidents with the guests and it seemed to be the last straw. Dad sort of … I don't know … went to pieces really. So did this place as a result. Dad's spent a long time just shuffling around and not really connecting with things. The fact that he asked you to come up is actually a really good sign that he might be getting back into things."

"Oh right," said Rory, cringing at how wrong his first set of ideas had been and feeling a new pressure to get things right.

"I just do my own thing a lot of the time. I get loads of time for painting which is what I want to do anyway, so I suppose it works out okay for me."

"Do you think things will ever change?" asked Rory.

"That depends a bit on you, doesn't it?" asked Grimson. Rory looked away embarrassed at the thought that his pretence with Zizz Cola was seen as the basis for a route out of trouble. "I think the old Dad is still in there. I reckon he'll appear again some day, but in recent years it's like he's been living in a cloud of sadness. That's the only way I can think of describing him."

Rory's found his mind in a spin. He was so used to hearing stories of Hotel Grimm and its owner from the playground and from *The Chronicle,* but here was a completely different picture being presented.

"I got it so completely wrong with my ideas for the hotel," he said in a doom-laden voice.

"Well, you wouldn't be the first and you probably won't be the last. Everyone thinks Dad's odd. He's just heartbroken. And he doesn't have it in him to fight back against all the stuff that rumbles on about him in the town."

"I ought to say sorry to him," said Rory.

"Well the best thing you could do would be to come up with something that gives him a new way of looking at things."

"I thought I had that, but I should have listened to Bonnie and Grandad."

"Well it must be hard to be a marketing genius all of the time," said Grimson with a grin.

Rory forced a weak smile.

"Come on," said Grimson. "I'd better show you out. You never know … if you stay here too long you might not make it out alive." His smile was mischievous but had a wisp of sadness through it. Rory shook his head, embarrassed not just at what he had presented at his meeting, but about the way the town had regarded Hotel Grimm over the years. He had a heavy heart as Grimson led the way confidently through the dim corridors and back down the stairs to the front door.

"So there's nothing else you think I ought to see in the hotel then?" asked Rory as they reached the exit.

"Not really," said Grimson. "You did the rounds with Grog the other day, and you've already done some exploring outside if you've been to the graveyard. I think you've pretty much seen the lot. I suppose you should see the pavilion …"

"Is that the wreck of a place down on the rock ledge?" asked Rory.

"Yeah," said Grimson. "It's been in that state for as long as I can remember. Apparently, it used to be where the wealthy guests strolled down to for afternoon tea. It used to be all posh and full of tables covered in white cloths. There were fish tanks around the walls and sun loungers outside on the ledge. So you've seen that too. Well in that case …"

A great big smile crossed Grimson's face. "I think you should take the easy way down the hill."

"What, jump?" said Rory, still feeling sorry for himself.

"Next best thing," said Grimson. "Take the cable car."

Before Rory could think of an excuse to match the anxious thoughts that flooded into his head, Grimson was off. He opened the hotel's front door and began striding down the steps. Some crows flew off a tree as his loping figure approached at speed. "Come on," he shouted over his shoulder. "I'll buzz Stobo and let him know it's needed."

"Don't look so scared," said Grimson as the cable car clanked into the station and came to a halt in front of them a few minutes later. "This will give you a chance to test out those telescopes I was telling you about. Who knows ... it could be the beginning of your own artistic career!"

Rory couldn't share the joke as he looked apprehensively at the cable car. Although he had seen it trundling away in the distance over the years without incident, the contraption was so linked to Hotel Grimm in his mind — and that of everyone else in Aberfintry — that no one would *ever* think of going in it.

"There's nothing to worry about," said Grimson, sensing his disquiet. "It's not the death trap it's cracked up to be. As long as you've got a good head for heights you'll be just fine."

"Do you know what, Rory ..." Grimson continued, seeing that he was hanging back. "You need to stop believing your own marketing campaign. We are not as weird as everyone thinks, or as freaky as you were probably planning on promoting us to be."

Rory didn't know what to say in response. He took another look at the cable car. "I'd love to go in it," he said.

"Nice one," said Grimson, his face beaming in a way that Rory hadn't seen before, as he strode over to the cable car station control desk, picked up a phone and waited briefly before speaking. "Hi, Stobo," he said. "Passenger heading your way when you're ready." Putting the phone down, Grimson clattered open the door and stood aside to let Rory step in.

"See you again soon, no doubt," said Grimson cheerily. "Have a nice trip!"

Rory watched as the door closed. As soon as it clicked shut he felt panic-stricken that he had made the wrong decision. The cable car seemed dangerously flimsy and he was very aware of being alone. It was only Grimson's smiling face on the other side of the glass that stopped him hammering on the door and wrenching on the handle to get out. He knew that anyone in the town would think he was out of his mind to risk his life in this way, but he had no more time to think about it as he watched Grimson push a large red button next to the phone. Seconds later the cable car moved smoothly away from the safety of the station.

Within seconds, the surface of Scrab Hill dropped away from below his feet and Rory was suspended in the metal and glass box making his way downhill. Looking to one side, he could see the graveyard where he had taken his wrong turning a week ago, the path down towards the ledge and the spot where he had sat to take in the view. Further below, Aberfintry sparkled in the sunshine like a picture with tiny moving pieces made up of people and cars and bikes. Rory remembered Grimson's words and headed for one of two telescopes set on stands by the windows. Rory could see how an instrument like this would give Grimson the tool he needed to study people. The powerful telescope immediately picked out Lachlan Stagg's statue so clearly that Rory could even make out features on the face.

Rory became so engrossed in scanning the town for the features he knew that he didn't notice that the cable car was approaching the end of its journey until it passed under the roof of the station at the bottom. Rory realized with a start that he was about to enter yet another zone that few in Aberfintry would consider doing lightly. After the calm of the journey his anxiety levels shot back up again. Whilst not as legendary as the hotel, the cable car station and Stobo were well known as things to avoid. Rory couldn't recall ever hearing of anyone who had actually set foot in the building that housed the machinery and the mechanic. But now, as the cable car left the open air and came to rest in the station, he was about to do just that.

“Quite simply, it feels like your life is hanging by a thread.”

Sir Gregory Grimm on the opening of the cable car (1946)

17. Stobo

Everyone in Aberfintry knew that the cable car station was the sole preserve of Stobo. The place was his, and his alone.With the cable car having been built to serve Hotel Grimm, their reputations went hand in hand. As such, children were warned to keep away from the wee man who had taken over as mechanic since the death of his father who had overseen the building and installation of the machinery.

One of the challenges at school was to see how close anyone dared to go to the cable car station, and as a further test of bravado to see how far they would go in provoking Stobo. Standard practice involved throwing stones on to the roof of the station. Being metal, the sharp bangs of the stones that landed on it sounded like bullets and for Stobo inside, it must have been like being under attack from the guns of a diving fighter plane. The stone throwing also extended to trying to pelt the cable car itself as it made occasional journeys up and down Scrab Hill. The competition wasn't just to try to hit the moving target, but to see who could still get a direct hit when the car was getting higher and higher and further and further out of range. Gordon Goodman famously held the record for smacking a small rock into the underside of the cable car just after it had passed the first pylon.

Now, Rory looked with concern through the window into the inside of the station. He felt trapped inside his own moving cell which had just delivered him to the heart of somewhere he didn't want to be. His eye was drawn to a plaque mounted beside the platform which passengers used to get on and off the cable car. It read: *"Constructed in 1946, this cable car was officially opened by Sir Gregory Grimm."*

It struck Rory that he had arrived into a piece of history that might contribute more to his understanding of Hotel Grimm. Maybe Stobo could unlock some of the secrets of the place, if he was prepared to do so?

Stepping tentatively out of the cable car and onto the platform, Rory could see that the station was in fact a giant workshop, which reminded him of his Grandad's one, although it was now at least a couple of years since he had been in there. Here everything was on a much larger scale. Large workbenches, containers full of spare parts, an entire substitute cable car on its side, lengths of cable and spare winding mechanisms and more tools than Rory had ever seen in his life neatly stored around the walls. As his gaze reached the back corner however, Rory could see that the station was more than a workshop. Through a half-open door Rory could make out a rumpled bed. It seemed that Stobo either lived at his work or worked where he lived. Rory wasn't quite sure which way round it was.

A scuff of a foot on the concrete floor made him realize with a start that there was a silent figure, hunched over at work in the far corner. There was only one person it could be, so taking a deep breath, Rory walked towards him. Stobo looked up as Rory approached and then turned his attention back to his work without any acknowledgement. At a glance it looked like he was working on Malky Mackay's black bike and Stobo continued to tinker with it as if Rory wasn't there.

Rory tried to look without staring. He had never seen such an oily man. Everything seemed coated in black grime from his flat cap, past his worn overalls, to his cracked stubby fingernails.

"Um … hi there," said Rory.

The clank of Stobo's spanner was the only noise that came in response. Rory paused and tried again.

"I was wondering if you had time to talk for a few minutes," he said hopefully. The same metallic sound was the only reply.

"I was interested in the cable car and wanted to find out a bit about it."

"Oh aye," said Stobo, continuing to work away, his face hidden from Rory.

"Can I ask you a few questions?" said Rory, trying to sound as polite as he could.

"Seems as though you've already started," said Stobo straightening up and moving over to a workbench to search for something.

"When was it all built?"

There was silence from Stobo leaving Rory unsure whether he had heard the question or not. Stobo continued to let his fingers rattle through a tin of nuts and bolts to find what he was after.

"You know the answer to that one already," said the mechanic after a long pause. "Facts like that are in books. What is it you really want to ask me?"

Rory paused. "Well, I suppose I'm interested in what it gets used for now ... you know, now that there aren't really any passengers coming and going."

"This and that," said Stobo.

"Is it all still in fine working order though?" asked Rory regretting the question as soon as it left his mouth. For the first time Stobo glanced at him and then looked away again. It was as if he was checking that Rory had asked a serious question.

"Do you think I would be wasting my time here if I didn't have it working?" said Stobo, finally finding what he was after and returning his attention to the bike. "It's as smooth as the day it was opened," he added.

"Were you around that day?" asked Rory spotting his opportunity to prise some more information out of the reticent man.

"Cheeky wee bandit. I'm not that old. My dad told me all about it though."

"What did he say?"

Again Stobo left a long pause. "There were people everywhere. Everyone in the town queuing up for a go. There had never been anything like it here or anywhere close to here."

"Did your Dad get to go on it that day?" asked Rory.

"Aye. Aye he did. The queues were enormous but Sir Gregory wanted him on there as a thank you.

And maybe just to check that it was actually working. Dad always said it was one of the best days he remembered in this place.

"Things a bit different now?" said Rory.

Stobo snorted and for a moment Rory thought that this was the only comment that he would give, but he continued. "Aye just a bit. It was once a curiosity or even something exotic in the town. Now it's just seen as part of the hotel and it's rubbished because of that."

"But you've done nothing wrong," said Rory.

"Neither have they," said Stobo with a fierce glare. Rory looked away embarrassed.

"So what *does* it get used for now? What kind of 'this and that?'" asked Rory before Stobo had a chance just to repeat his earlier answer.

"Well let's just say we do more goods than passenger transport now."

"Things to keep the hotel going?" asked Rory.

"Food goes up," said Stobo, "... and some of it comes back down again cooked."

"You get some of Ramsay's food?"

"I do. He looks after me very well."

"Is it as good as he says?"

"Probably better I would say," said Stobo, his mood lifting.

"Do you get frustrated that it's only used for carting stuff up and down the hill?" asked Rory.

Stobo seemed to ignore the question. "What did you think of your journey?"

"It was great," said Rory. "Over too quickly I suppose. Those telescopes are brilliant." There was a longer than usual pause from Stobo. When he did speak it was softer and more quietly.

"Well there's your answer. It's a beautiful thing this machine, not something to be feared. It should be doing what it was made to do. It would have broken my dad's heart if he knew what had happened here."

"At least you're still caring for it. I mean still looking after what he built. He'd be pleased about that."

For the first time Stobo looked at Rory. He gave a short appreciative nod. "Aye, son, aye I think he would be."

A buzz went off in Rory's backpack as his mobile phone announced that a text had been received.

18. Never known but never forgotten

Can u meet me?
Sat 1pm. Gates of
Park St cemetery.
Something to
show u. B

It hadn't taken long for Rory to say goodbye to Stobo. The man's monosyllabic style had not lent itself to a long drawn-out farewell. Leaving the cable car station and walking back into town he stared again at the text. The good news was that Bonnie was still communicating with him. The bad news was that visiting another graveyard wasn't really Rory's favoured way of spending a Saturday afternoon. However, not only had Bonnie's view about his plan for the hotel been correct, but the last time she had asked him to look at something had led to meeting Grimson at the mural. Rory concluded that her recent track record of good judgment meant that the Park Street Cemetery had to be his next stop.

Rory's fear was that he would have to spend a long time reliving his disastrous meeting at Hotel Grimm, but that was short-lived. Perhaps the fact that he had greeted Bonnie by saying "You were right and I was wrong" had helped.

"I know," said Bonnie, sounding unsurprised and unperturbed. "Hopefully there's not too much damage done. You'll need to tell me everything you saw today, but in the meantime, I've been doing some work behind the scenes. Follow me," she said pushing the joystick on her chair forward and buzzing off. Rory dutifully trooped along behind her.

The gates of the cemetery led them into a narrow tree-lined road which wound its way between a series of low hills with neat rows of gravestones. Bonnie appeared to know exactly where she was headed. "It's that one," she said stopping abruptly at another block of stones that to Rory looked the same as all the others. "It's the one at this end of the third row. Have a look."

In the silence of the graveyard, Rory stepped closer, finding that he was almost doing it on tiptoes. Not knowing why Bonnie had brought him here, Rory shivered as he approached the grave that Bonnie had pointed him towards. There were some fresh flowers on it and there was a small card pinned to them. Rory looked at the words on the stone. "Much loved daughter and sister. Died Tragically". It was Lottie Gilchrist's grave. For someone who had died in 1948, the gravestone looked remarkably well kept. Rory leaned in and peered closely at the card on the flowers, not wanting to pick them up and disturb the scene.

For Auntie. Never known but never forgotten.

DG.

Rory tried to work out what he was seeing. "Who's been looking after this?" he said out loud.

"Presumably a Gilchrist," said Bonnie. "The surname begins with G."

"I thought Grandad said that all of the Gilchrists moved out of town," said Rory.

"Maybe they come back to look after it," said Bonnie.

As Rory stood there pondering, the gathering breeze blew a piece of paper towards him and it stuck around his leg. Reaching down he peeled it off to find it was a page from the previous week's *Chronicle*. Crumpling it up, Rory looked around for a bin and then stopped dead. *The Chronicle.* Edited by Derek Goodman.

"Is this DG? Derek Goodman," asked Rory holding up the paper and showing Bonnie.

She looked unconvinced. "But why would Derek Goodman be calling Lottie Gilchrist "Auntie?" Surely your Grandad would have mentioned if there was a local link like that?"

"The card says "Never known but never forgotten"," said Rory. "Lottie Gilchrist died young, so Derek Goodman wouldn't have known her." He hadn't worked it all out but something felt like it was falling into place. With determination Rory turned and began to stride back up the cemetery's narrow road.

"Oi, wait for me Zizz Boy," said Bonnie, whizzing her wheelchair into life to catch up with him. "Where are you going?"

"I think that Grandad has got a bit of explaining to do," Rory shouted back to her. "I think he's been playing a few cards just a little too close to his chest." There was a hint of anger in Rory's voice.

Leaving the gates and still walking fast, Rory marched down the road away from the cemetery, crossing over the bridge before heading up the hill in to the town. Oblivious to Bonnie's cries for him to slow down, it was only as they reached Aberfintry's main street that she managed to catch him.

"Stop for a minute would you?" she said. "Give me a chance, Rory. Top speed on this can't quite keep up with you when you're in that sort of a mood." Rory mumbled an apology as he slowed down.

"We need to think things through properly before we speak to your Grandad," said Bonnie. "Also, you've not even told me what happened this morning up at the hotel, although you're probably avoiding that. Did it go as badly as I think it did?"

"Sorry," said Rory. "My head's just spinning at the moment." He plonked himself down on a bench and ran through the events of the morning. Bonnie was not surprised to hear Granville Grimm's reaction but she was amazed to hear about a bathroom full of Grog's pets, a portrait of her in Grimson's room, and the fact that Rory had returned on the cable car. "I've always wanted a ride on that, right from when I was little," she said.

Bonnie's voice tailed off as she looked over Rory's shoulder with a quizzical expression. "Who is that weird looking guy?"

A man had emerged from the library and was checking the contents of his carrier bag. As he set off walking, his limping gait was unmistakable.

"What is *he* doing here?" said Rory.

"He's not the butler guy you've mentioned, is he?" asked Bonnie.

"The one and the same," said Rory, trying to imagine what could possibly have brought Grog into town. At that moment, there was some shouting from nearby.

"Heh ... what have we got here?"

"I think someone ... or something ... has escaped from Hotel Grimm!"

"Don't go near ... you might just drop down dead."

Gordon and Gracie Goodman had emerged from a side street and were approaching Grog with mischievous curiosity. At first, Grog was oblivious to comments being directed at him, but Gordon and Gracie edged closer and closer, leaving him in no doubt that he had been targetted.

"Heh. What are you doing in *our* town?"

"Yeah, get back where you belong."

Grog kept his head down and did his best to carry on walking. For a split second, the thought of slipping quietly away and avoiding this messy situation, passed through Rory's mind, but he dismissed it.

"Where is Malky Mackay when you need him?" Rory muttered, getting off the bench and jogging over to where the incident was unfolding.

"Leave him alone you two."

"Watch out!" said Gracie turned, pretending to be afraid. "Zizz Boy is here!" Gordon took a swipe at Grog's carrier bag. It fell to the ground spilling books.

"Oh no, you've dropped your things," Gordon said with mock concern.

He reached down and picked up a book. *"Looking after Reptiles?* Trying to take better care of yourself?" he mocked.

"Leave me alone," croaked Grog as he struggled to bend down and get the books.

"Do as he says. Leave him alone," said Bonnie, arriving at the scene.

"Oh no!" said Gracie throwing her hands up in horror. "There's two of them! Zizz Boy and The Worm. We don't stand a chance Gordon!"

"Find something better to do, Gracie," said Bonnie. "What's he done to you?"

"He's from up there isn't he?" hissed Gracie Goodman. Her finger stabbed the air and pointed towards Hotel Grimm.

"He's got as much right to be here as you have," retorted Bonnie.

"Not after what that place has done," Gracie spat back.

Rory picked up the last of Grog's books and helped him get them back into his bag. The man looked Rory in the eye and gave him a firm nod of thanks.

"Why should you care anyway, Zizz Boy?" said Gordon, turning his attention to Rory. Spotting his chance, Grog slipped quietly away.

"He's trying to make up for the past, isn't he?" said Gracie.

Rory felt the heat build in his face. Surely they didn't know about the Zizz slogan? If the Goodman twins found out that he wasn't responsible for that, it would be far worse than the ribbing he got for having become the Zizz Boy.

"Gone all quiet on us now, hasn't he," said Gracie.

"Got something to hide, Zizz Boy?" chipped in Gordon.

"Come on, Rory," said Bonnie. "Let's not waste our time here." She headed off giving Rory a cue to follow her. The jeers floated through the air behind them.

"Aww ... they make such a lovely couple."

"She's got the brains ... he's got the ... What has he got exactly?"

"What was all that about?" asked Bonnie when they were out of earshot. "Making up for the past and having something to hide."

"Don't look at me," said Rory still prickling from the exchange. "Remember it's Grandad who's not been telling us everything he knows," he added, stalking off towards Boglehole Road.

“Bringing You The News You Need About Your Town”

Strapline for The Chronicle

19. Confrontation at *The Chronicle*

"Keep your hair on. Keep your hair on," said Grandad, as Rory strode into the living room at 47 Boglehole Road asking questions without giving any time for answers. Before they could go any further, they were interrupted by thumping and muffled shouting from the other side of the front door. In his desperation to interrogate his Grandad, Rory had let the front door bang shut leaving Bonnie unable to get into the house. Red-faced, Rory backtracked to let her in.

"Imagine forgetting your partner in crime," said Grandad with a grin.

"We've not committed any crime, but we'll have you for withholding information from the investigation," said Rory, frustrated that his opening salvo of questions had been cut short.

"That's a serious charge," said Grandad winking at Bonnie and looking for some back-up. This time she gave him nothing in support.

"Now where were we?" said Grandad. "Oh aye. You were standing in front of me having completely lost the plot. I hope you're going to be a bit calmer second time round. I suggest you just give me one question at a time and I'll see what I can do."

Rory took a deep breath, which was the only gap that Bonnie needed to beat him to it. "Why are there fresh flowers on Lottie Gilchrist's grave? Was she Derek Goodman's Auntie? Are the initials 'DG' for Derek Goodman or is there some Gilchrist in town we didn't know about?"

"Och, don't you start!" said Grandad. "I might just put my head under my blanket and hope that you'll go away! What is this all about? Where have you two just come from?"

"We've just been to Park Street Cemetery," said Bonnie.

"You pair know how to have a good time, don't you? Aren't kids like you supposed to be playing with computers or vandalizing bus shelters or something?"

"Come on, Grandad," said Rory. "Quit the smart comments and just give us some answers. Lottie Gilchrist. Who was she? I mean who might she have become? I mean …"

"What are you talking about?" said Grandad.

Rory explained about Lottie's grave, the flowers, the note and the initials "DG."

"Right … I'm with you now. The Gilchrists did move away decades ago, so the initials are nothing to do with them. But Detectives McKenna and O'Donnell are correct in making a link to Derek Goodman."

"I knew it!" said Rory clapping his hands together as Bonnie gave an appreciative nod. "What's the connection?" she said.

"Well, if you give me a minute, I'm coming to that." Grandad heaved himself to get more upright in his seat. "Hunter Goodman, who used to manage *The Chronicle* by the way, married a woman called Nancy Gilchrist and they had a son, called Derek."

"So who was Lottie Gilchrist?" asked Bonnie.

"Nancy's twin sister. They were identical and very close. In fact, Nancy never really got over the death of her sister. She died just a few years later and everyone said it was from a broken heart."

"So that means that Derek Goodman, or 'DG,' lost his mum when he was young because his Aunt Lottie that he never knew died in that accident," said Rory. "You could have told us that, Grandad."

"I didn't think it mattered that much," said Grandad, "I can't see what you're trying to prove, Rory."

Bonnie piped up. "Well if Derek Goodman is still leaving flowers to this day on the grave of a woman he never knew it's obviously important to him. If he thinks that someone, or something like Hotel Grimm, is to blame for that fact ..."

"Then who knows what kind of stuff he is going to write about them?" said Rory completing the thought.

Grandad wasn't keen on the idea, but Rory and Bonnie reckoned it had to be the next step, and a simple call set up an immediate appointment at *The Chronicle's* office.

"I'm sorry," said Rory to Bonnie after he put the phone down. "I can picture the place. It's upstairs."

"That's rubbish," she said. "I think I'll write a letter of complaint to the paper. Do you think they'll print it?" she asked with a mischievous grin.

After parting company with Bonnie, Rory considered how ironic it was that the history of Hotel Grimm was so closely linked to the paper. *The Chronicle* declared every week that it wanted the place closed but it seemed that the paper would be a bit lost without its favourite front page story. If the hotel ever did close, maybe *The Chronicle* would need to look at its own rebranding, Rory thought ruefully. Turning the last corner, he bumped straight into his mother.

"Rory! Fancy meeting you here," said Momo, flapping in the usual flurry of baggy coloured clothes and jewellery that could double as percussion instruments.

"Hi Mum, what are you doing here?" said Rory.

"Well, I've just been at *The Chronicle* seeing if they would do a feature on my next exhibition. I must say Derek Goodman was charming and I think he's going to be very supportive. It's all very exciting Rory. It's called "Half Measures". You see, imagine if ..."

"Er ... actually, Mum, I've got to go *The Chronicle* too, and I don't want to be late."

"Now you see, Rory, this is a bit of what 'Half Measures' is about. We are all in such a rush these days that we need to slow down a bit. We'll get twice as much back you know!"

"Yeah, okay," said Rory, "But right now I really *am* in a rush. Maybe see you later?"

"I'll be at the studio later, but there's stuff in the fridge for tea." Rory sometimes had difficulty making out if the fridge contents were to be eaten or were some of his mother's art materials. Half measures was often what he ended up taking to start with, just to be on the safe side.

"Great thanks. Must dash, Mum."

The brass plaque to the side of the door read "The Chronicle: serving Aberfintry since 1908." As he reached the top of the stairs, a receptionist looked up from behind her desk. Rory couldn't think at first why her severely pulled-back hair and glasses were familiar to him. Then he realized that he had seen her portrait that morning. Grimson had seen something not immediately obvious to Rory as it had suggested a warmth that the woman herself did not seem to possess. The nameplate on her desk said she was Deirdre Dunbar, which was more of an introduction than she was ever going to make herself.

"Yes?" and a raised eyebrow were as much as Rory got for a welcome.

"Er … Rory McKenna to see Derek Goodman."

Deirdre Dunbar gave a curt nod to indicate that Rory should sit in one of two seats by the window. Rory looked around the walls at the framed *Chronicle* front pages representing decades of local reporting. The first headline he noticed was, *"He's Done it Again!!!"* with a photo of Lachlan Stagg driving a JCB that was almost failing to hold an enormous and presumably world-record-breaking potato in its giant scoop. Glancing further around the reception area he could see that at least half a dozen of the pages were reporting some outrage connected with Hotel Grimm. He could only make out the headline and subtext detail of the one nearest to him. *"Inferno at Hotel Grimm" American tourist and staff member recovering in hospital.*

Rory strained to see more but felt that getting up from his seat to look more closely would somehow be frowned upon by Deirdre Dunbar. As it was, he managed to annoy her anyway because he was concentrating so hard on trying to read at a distance, that he didn't notice her telling him that he could go through to see Derek Goodman. Caught out, Rory suddenly felt very unprepared to see the editor but headed for the indicated door, knocked and entered.

"Good afternoon, Rory. What a coincidence, having just seen your mother," said Derek Goodman rising from his desk with a thin smile and an outstretched hand. "The whole town feels it knows you so well but it's good to finally meet you in person. Of course, I have my own sources, as Gracie and Gordon have told me so much about you."

Rory winced and wondered what on earth the gruesome twosome would have said about him.

"So how are things in the world of Zizz Cola?" he said, indicating for Rory to sit in the chair on the other side of his desk. "Is there some exciting update that *The Chronicle* should know about?"

"Things are fine thanks, but that's not really the reason I'm here."

"Sounds intriguing. Tell me more," said Goodman, reaching for a pen and a spiral bound notebook.

"I've actually been doing a bit of local history

investigation and thought that you may be able to help out," said Rory.

"Local history, eh?" said Goodman sounding slightly disappointed. "Well *The Chronicle* has certainly been covering stories for a few decades, so we may be able to comment."

"Yes," said Rory. "I've actually been using your archive in the library."

"Excellent," said Derek Goodman. "Being a resource to the community is what we are all about. So what brings you here now?"

"I thought that it might help to talk to you directly," said Rory, feeling increasingly anxious about how to raise what he was here to talk about.

"How flattering," said Goodman, "What particular topic is it you're interested in?"

"Hotel Grimm," said Rory.

"Oh really?" said Goodman his face impassive and his voice flat. The only change in his manner was that although the editor looked straight at Rory, his pen began to write slowly across the page of the pad in front of him, almost as if his hand was disconnected from the rest of him.

"Yes," said Rory, concentrating on looking Goodman straight in the eye and holding his gaze. "*The Chronicle* has certainly given a lot of coverage to the place over the years."

"Well…" said Goodman. "It's made its own coverage really." His face seemed to go from cold to frozen. "Unfortunately, there are just so many disastrous things that continue to happen there. We've just been the ones to report it and make sure that everyone nearby knows exactly what's happening on their doorstep." His pen raised and hovered over the page like a hawk. "What is it you're interested in exactly, may I ask?"

"I suppose ... well, in all the reading I've been doing ... I find that ... I'm just trying to separate fact from fiction," said Rory.

There was a long pause. Derek Goodman's eyes seemed to be boring into him and Rory found that he couldn't keep looking at the editor any longer. His eyes flickered away and when Goodman spoke it was with barely veiled anger. "Separate fact from fiction? I do *not* like what you are implying there. You should be careful with your choice of phrase. What makes you think there is fiction in the contents of *The Chronicle?*"

"Well," said Rory beginning to wish that Bonnie was sitting beside him to give him some backup. "I was wondering if there could have been another way of looking at what has happened at Hotel Grimm, that didn't cast the hotel in quite the same negative light?" Even as he spoke Rory felt like he was digging a huge hole that he was on the verge of falling into.

"Go on," said Goodman.

"There are things that you seem to have missed out. Like the fact that Gwendolen Grimm died a few years ago," suggested Rory. "A real tragedy for the Grimm family, but not one that you seem to have reported in any way at all."

There was a pause. "Mmm," said Goodman thoughtfully, the hint of a smile returning to his face. "What an interesting visit this is turning out to be. What *is* this meeting really about, I wonder?

The world famous Zizz Boy comes to see me to talk about Hotel Grimm and to claim that things aren't so bad up there after all. What *is* going on? Don't tell me that you're involved with the Grimms?"

Rory was disconcerted to see that Goodman's pen was now flying across the page even though the man continued to stare intently at Rory. It was too far away and too upside down for Rory to see what was being written but he was becoming very nervous about it.

Goodman meanwhile was like a fox with a first decent sniff of a rabbit; his smile widening with every breath.

"They've got to you haven't they?" he said.

"Got to me?" said Rory confused at Goodman's remark.

"Yes, yes, yes. That evil murdering crew. They've wheedled away at you with a sob story, lured you into believing that they're something they're not, and now here you are trying to separate *fact* from *fiction*." Goodman's fingers flicked the air to signify his use of Rory's phrase.

As Goodman's confidence and smile grew by the second, Rory began to bristle with anger. "No one has got to me," he snapped, flicking his fingers back in the same way. "I can make my own judgement about things."

"The global success has gone to your head." Goodman's pen stopped writing and he leaned over the desk towards Rory. The smile faded and he lowered his voice. "Let me tell you, young man, that place is dangerous and it *will* close. Oh yes … I will see to it personally."

Before Rory could stop himself, the stony face of the editor provoked him too much. He snapped back and everything spilled out. “You really don’t like the Grimms, do you? You have a grudge and you get a dig in at every opportunity. Is it because of what happened to Lottie Gilchrist and your mother? You’ve just never been able to forgive them?”

There was a long long silence and Derek Goodman seemed unable to look directly at Rory as his eyes cast around looking for a place to land. Then they narrowed and he gave Rory a piercing look.

“So you’re going to make this personal are you? Why should you care anyway, Zizz Boy? What is it you’re trying to do up there? Trying to make amends?”

“What do you mean make amends?” Rory asked.

“For the fact that your family is at the root of the problems.” Goodman spat the words out and sat back.

“I really don’t know what you are talking about,” said Rory, genuinely perplexed and trying to think how his parents might have influenced events at Hotel Grimm.

Goodman shook his head and gave Rory a contemptuous look. “Playing the innocent even though all of the deaths could probably be laid at your own family’s front door.”

Rory shook his head. “You have completely lost me.”

“The Curse of the Stonemason ... it’s all to do with your Grandad.” Rory looked at Derek

Goodman with bewilderment. At that moment, it dawned on Derek Goodman that he was giving information to Rory that the boy knew nothing of, and his amused smirk returned. "Well, well, well." The words came out slowly and each one delivered with relish. "We really are in the business of telling people the news here, aren't we? I can hardly believe that you don't know. You've got skeletons in your closet, Rory McKenna and pretty big ones at that."

Rory was speechless. He had nothing left to reply with.

"The Curse of the Stonemason," repeated Goodman. "You need to ask your Grandad about his stone-carving career and why it was so short-lived."

Rory tumbled out of the seat without a word and walked out of *The Chronicle's* office in a daze.

curse n. an appeal for evil or misfortune to befall someone or something

Dictionary definition

20. The curse of the Stonemason

Bonnie was waiting outside for Rory as planned and found him in a state of confusion. When he could finally explain what had happened at *The Chronicle* office, he was keener than ever to have sharp words with his Grandad. Bonnie pleaded with him not to rush in. "There must be more background information we can find out before we land this on him. Let's face it, if he's not telling us everything then it might be more productive to do some research elsewhere first." Since they were near to the library she was able to reason with Rory further that some of the facts were almost at their fingertips. Rory had to grudgingly admit that Bonnie was right, even though he was anxious to get to Boglehole Road.

Mrs Trinder-Kerr looked distinctly unimpressed that *two* people now wanted to look at *The Chronicle* archive, and her face soured still further as Bonnie also requested a copy of Lachlan Stagg's book on Hotel Grimm's stone carvings and gargoyles. She gave Bonnie a look as if to say she had expected better of her. Checking *The Chronicle* index gave them a few references to the Curse of the Stonemason, but the related articles didn't give the detail of the story that they were after. They soon realized that it was Lachlan Stagg's book that had the information they wanted, and they both fell silent as Bonnie turned to the chapter entitled "The History of the Curse."

The Curse of the Stonemason dates back to the late 1940s when much of the decorative work was being undertaken on Hotel Grimm. At that time the workforce is estimated to have been forty men at any one time, and included stonemasons from around Scotland. This group was supplemented by local Aberfintry men, and also by boys who had just left school. They gained work experience and apprenticeships in a way that no other project in the area could have provided in the post-war years. The story of the Curse of the Stonemason revolves around one of these schoolboys. As with all of the young lads, Hugh Munro was given bits and pieces of work to do to start with, typically fetching and carrying for the more experienced men, but such were the demands of Sir Gregory Grimm's plans for intricate designs throughout the hotel, that many of the boys moved onto stone-carving work, learning the skill on the job. Hugh Munro cut his stone-carving teeth on some of the gargoyles on the north tower and then on the figure-head over the front door. Those who worked alongside him reflect now that, right from the start, Munro was a prodigious talent, and the experienced men were soon happy to leave him to carve complicated pieces. Munro's appetite for a challenge was also there and he was drafted in to some of the jobs that required the greatest head for heights.

The story of the Curse revolves around a piece that was destined to remain firmly on the ground. Sir Gregory Grimm was keen to have the family emblem of a snarling wolf brought to life in the form of a giant statue that he wanted to place just inside the main door of the hotel as a spectacular welcome for every guest. The early stages of the statue were being worked on by master stonemason, Fraser Dalyell, who took it on as a personal project. However, Dalyell fell ill and was off site for a month. As time pressures grew, and an opening date was scheduled for the hotel, the young apprentice, Hugh Munro, took over. He became so absorbed in the task that he is reputed to have worked on it day and night. In fact, the story goes that when Dalyell eventually returned, the statue was finished and the exhausted Munro was asleep beside it. The statue was so amazing, so life-like and such an example of remarkable stonemasonry that Dalyell flew into a rage of professional jealousy. He was so incensed that he stormed away from the hotel refusing to touch another stone. His final act was to hurl his tools at the wolf, breaking off the tongue and three of its front teeth and screaming that a curse would befall the Grimm family, the hotel and those connected with the statue. Dalyell was never seen again. Those who witnessed Dalyell's fury said that ....

"Time's up," said a sharp voice behind them. Mrs Trinder-Kerr stood with arms folded. "We're closing. It's Saturday. We close early."

"But ...!" said Rory and Bonnie simultaneously, knowing that they had just unearthed a new treasure chest of information. Rory started to plead. "Can we take ...?"

"No," snapped Mrs Trinder-Kerr. "Reference book. No, you cannot take it home."

Bonnie and Rory left the library together, deeply frustrated and reeling from what they had just read. As they talked over what Lachlan Stagg's book had revealed, they agreed that they could not put off a trip to Grandad's any longer.

"This might be difficult stuff for him to talk about, Rory," Bonnie warned him.

"Well, he'll just have to," said Rory feeling little sympathy. "This could be a life or death matter for me if I don't get my facts straight about the hotel."

"Sounds like it nearly was for him too," said Bonnie. Her attempts to get him to take it easy, fell on deaf ears. Rory managed at least to make his usual entrance into Boglehole Road with the cry of "It's me," but the niceties were out of the way as soon as they got into the living room.

"Who did you take to the ball?" asked Rory.

"Eh?" said Grandad looking up from his armchair and casting a glance at Bonnie for help.

"Come on, Grandad, you heard me," said Rory.

Hugh Munro looked uncomfortable. "Well first things first. Can you shift these cushions? My back is really beginning to play up." Rory could see that Grandad was a bit ill at ease but it didn't seem like the usual stiffness. He did as he was asked, but reckoning that Grandad had let the question slip by, he repeated it.

"So who did you take to the ball then, Grandad?"

"Ach, son, it was a long time ago. A man of my age can't mind everything, you know."

"Come on Grandad. That's not the sort of thing you would forget. Who was it? I can cope if it wasn't Gran, you know. I suppose it might have been before the two of you got together."

Grandad cleared his throat and continued to squirm in his seat. He was looking less and less comfortable by the minute. As he watched the old man, Rory was struck by sharp pang of guilt. Here he was pushing his Grandad to open up and be honest, and feeling hurt that the old man might not have told him everything he could, while he himself was still holding on to his own big secret, with no plan to let anyone know.

Rory realized that the colour had drained from the old man's face and his breathing didn't sound quite right. Now feeling more concerned than anything else, Rory asked, "Are you alright, Grandad?"

"Aye, son … just give me a wee minute and I'll be fine." Grandad fiddled with his collar and took a deep breath.

Grandad's "wee minute" seemed to take a few, during which Rory and Bonnie exchanged wordless glances.

"Right, son, there's something I should tell you," said Grandad. He was sitting more comfortably although he still looked tense and drawn. He looked off to the side as he spoke, seemingly unable to meet Rory or Bonnie's gaze. "The truth of the matter is that I did take someone to the dance that night." His voice faltered, "But well, I suppose I wish now that I hadn't. I took a girl who I'd been seeing a wee bit of. It was maybe the third time we had done something together." Grandad's chin trembled and his voice began to falter. "It was Lottie Gilchrist."

It was Rory's turn to feel the colour drain from his face. He felt his mouth go dry and his brain begin to whirl. His Grandad was still looking away from him, and looked like he had aged ten years in the last two minutes. Rory could barely raise a whisper. "It was you with her up on the roof that night?"

"Aye, it was. The worst night of my life."

"It must have been awful, Mr Munro," said Bonnie. "I'm so sorry."

"Ach, it's in the past now. It's just not the easiest thing to speak about, even after all this time."

Rory had gone very quiet. Inside he was boiling with questions and unable to help himself, they all spilled out.

"So what else is there, Grandad? What about the Curse of the Stonemason? We've just found out about that one too. What's all this about you being an expert stonemason? The Curse came out because of your work didn't it? Did Lottie die because of your wolf statue and Fraser Dalyell's curse?" he said, far more sharply than perhaps he meant to.

"Rory!" hissed Bonnie.

"What?" he snapped back.

She gave him a look as if to say "Back off!!"

"Well things keep coming up that you've deliberately not told us, Grandad. How can we expect to get the answers we need, if you keep secrets from us? I mean is there anything else you're hiding?"

The accusation was out before Rory even realized what he was saying, but he was finding it so frustrating that someone, who was supposed to be helping him was keeping so much to himself. Grandad didn't say anything. He just sat there looking very very tired, and nodding slowly as if processing what Rory had just said.

As the silence continued, Rory began to feel bad. He had never spoken to his Grandad like that before and it didn't feel like a good place to be. He felt he had to speak first.

"Listen, Grandad, I'm sorry. That was a bit out of order. I'm just really worried about all of this stuff and I thought … I thought I knew everything there was to know about you."

"No, you're right, son, you're quite right," said Grandad. "It's not fair on you. There is something else and it's high time I told you about it. Time to stop hiding away."

Rory looked at his Grandad. Given the recent revelations, he couldn't begin to think what was going to come out next.

"You know my workshop, Rory? Well, there's something that you should maybe have a look at. The door at the back. The one I always said was my own wee place. Well take a look in there. It might help to explain the way things have been over the years."

Momentarily confused, Rory then remembered the door at the far side of the workshop which had been out of bounds all of the time he had spent there. Grandad struggled to his feet ignoring the protests from Rory and Bonnie, and with great effort shuffled to the back door of the house, his slippers squeaking on the kitchen linoleum. He reached for two keys on a hook, peering at them to make sure they were the right ones. "This was always going to happen some day," he said handing them to Rory and opening the door to the garden. "I just didn't know if I'd be alive to see it. Take these and go and have a look."

Stepping out of the back door and down the steps, Rory walked along the long path to the bottom of the garden as if on a journey back in time. It soon became clear that with his Grandad now living life indoors, the garden that he knew so well from the past had been lost. The once neat flowerbeds were bare and the grass leading down the slope towards the workshop was long and unkempt.

A pile of leaves had gathered against the base of the workshop door and ivy had begun to grow around the hinges. Rory crunched the first key into the rusting padlock. It took a few twists and a squeak of protest before it turned and the lock grudgingly opened. The wood had warped over the years and Rory had to tug hard to get the door to budge. As it creaked open, cobwebs tore and spiders scrabbled away as the first rays of light filtered in to the workshop. Inside, unused tools were covered in a thick layer of dust, cardboard boxes had collapsed, and the holes in the old armchair that Rory used to sit on suggested that a family of mice had moved in to it. Rory's nose wrinkled as long forgotten smells came back to him.

Taking the second key and brushing past more cobwebs, Rory headed for the back of the workshop and the door that he had never been through before. It was another tough job to get the lock working but with a heave on the handle and his shoulder to the frame, he shoved it open. Rory fumbled for a light switch. It clunked down and a strip light flickered, once, twice, three times and then on. Rory stood motionless, faced by a roomful of animals staring at him.

Grimm is burning, Grimm is burning,
Fire Fire, Fire Fire
Just ignore it, just ignore it,
Don't bring water, don't bring water

Singing round

21. Finkleman and the fire

Deer, foxes, squirrels, rabbits, hedgehogs, owls and many more creatures sat on the workshop floor; every one of them beautifully carved in stone and larger than life. Details of paws and claws, feathers, fur and whiskers were all carefully ground out of grey granite. The tools that had shaped the animals, hammers of different weights and chisels of varying sizes, lay neatly in rows on a workbench, relics of another era. Rory moved among the animals almost expecting that brushing against them might bring them to life. His mind turned over and over. All of these years and this collection being painstakingly chiselled, carved and polished by his Grandad working alone, for the finished sculptures to sit unseen by anyone. How much of the time as he created each animal had he spent thinking of the Stonemason's Curse? Or even of Lottie Gilchrist? That was surely the reason why this work had never seen the light of day; a fear that anything else he created might have similar deadly consequences.

Rory looked more closely at the first row of animals. They were brilliant. He couldn't help thinking of his mother in recent years with her exhibitions of household objects and statements of the obvious to go with them. Here was the real talent in the family but no one even knew about it. It seemed such a waste. He felt a creeping sense of embarrassment at the fact that he was falsely thought of as a genius, when here were the results of decades of his Grandad's creativity right in front of him.

The animals were stacked a few deep right across the width of the room and on a rough count Rory could see at least fifty. It felt like he was standing in some kind of stone-sculptured Noah's Ark. He wanted to stay and try to take it all in, but deep down he knew that what he really wanted was to see his Grandad again.

As he reached the back door, he could hear raised voices at the front of the house. Going through the kitchen he found both Bonnie and Grandad in the hall having just closed the front door.

"I reckon the heat might be about to be turned up on the hotel, Rory," said Bonnie.

"What's happened?" said Rory.

"There was a bit of a commotion outside. People running past. So we went to check it out. Sounds like Gracie and Gordon have pushed Stobo just a little too far."

"Aye, the wee man has struck back. Quite right too if you ask me," said Grandad working his slow way back into the living room and easing himself into his armchair.

"They were on a dare to go right inside a cable car," explained Bonnie. "Probably planning to leave something horrible in there. Anyway, Stobo spotted them coming so he left them to it, but as soon as they were in the car, he closed the doors and set it off a few hundred metres, then stopped it."

Rory couldn't help but smile at the thought of Gracie and Gordon suspended in mid-air high above Scrab Hill, with no hint of when they might get down.

"Anyway," continued Bonnie. "It seems that Gracie had her mobile phone so of course she immediately called her Dad who went absolutely ballistic and came down at ninety miles an hour to sort things out. He's coming out with all sorts of accusations of kidnapping children and assault."

"Aye, but good on Donald Stobo," said Grandad chuckling. "Apparently he said, "If I wanted to kidnap someone they would be the last people I would want to spend time with … and why would anyone want to pay a ransom for them anyway?""

"So where are they now?" said Rory.

"Back down on the ground," said Bonnie. "That was them all heading back into town there. Gracie and Gordon were both bubbling their eyes out. Apparently Gordon's not that good with heights."

"What a laugh!" said Rory. "It's brilliant they're getting a taste of their own medicine."

"Yeah, but what's *The Chronicle* going to do about this, Rory?" asked Bonnie. "Stand by for the backlash. I think your job might be about to get harder."

As they settled down again, Rory got the chance to explain to Bonnie and speak to his Grandad about the secrets of the workshop.

"Sorry I spoke to you like that, Grandad. The things you've done down there are just amazing."

His Grandad spoke a little about why he had worked away in secret over the years.

"I loved my work at the park," he said, "but my real love was working in stone. I just couldn't do it in public again though. I was too afraid after what happened up at the hotel. If anybody else had been harmed, I'd never have forgiven myself."

It seemed as though the events of the last hour had worn Grandad out and after a short time Bonnie gave Rory a nod to suggest that they should leave the old man alone for a while. They left the house talking about some of the day's long list of events. Rory could hardly believe it was only that morning he had been up at the hotel.

Whilst all of the stories from Grandad's younger days were incredible, what was increasingly troubling him was the fact that a Curse did seem to have been the start of the Hotel's problems.

"Just how am I supposed to come up with something that beats that?" asked Rory.

"All these things could still just be coincidence and misfortune, Rory," said Bonnie. "You've said it yourself. You can look at things in a different light. Nothing has happened to you from all the contact you've had with the place."

Not yet, thought Rory.

Looking forward to a quiet evening, Rory returned home to find that his day of unfolding stories had not yet come to an end. As he came in the door there was a shout from his mum.

"Rory! Call for you!"

Going into the kitchen he found Momo McKenna on the phone with a huge dippy smile on her face. "That's him here now," she spoke into the phone,

"I'll hand you over."

She put her hand over the receiver and whispered in a far too loud voice. "Don't worry I've been keeping him occupied for the last wee while! It's that nice American, Mr Finkleman. I think he might be interested in sponsoring my exhibition!" Rory looked at her in despair as he grabbed the phone.

"Hi, Mr Finkleman, it's Rory here."

"Heh there, buddy … how's it going? Just had a great little talk with your mom. Boy, she's a character, huh? Must be great fun to live with."

"Er yeah … quite … um … unusual."

"Listen, buddy, I needed to touch base with you about a few things. There is some Zizz business, or *Zizzness* as the marketing guys are calling it now, to attend to soon. I think China is going to be massive for us and the guys over there are interested in your story."

Rory's head slumped. *Not more publicity, please!* he thought.

Finkleman continued. "But the real reason for this call though is that I wanted to let you know about this bizarre family coincidence I mentioned in my e-mail. When I met you at the café on my holiday all that time ago, I had bought a bunch of postcards of your pretty little town. Anyways, the way things went after I met you it was months before I actually got round to sending them. When I did, one of them went to my Aunt Agatha in Wisconsin. Turns out, not only has she been to Aberfintry years ago — and I'm talking *years* ago — but, wait for it, she says she owes her life to some guy in your town! She was very insistent that if I ever get to Scotland again I'm to hunt this guy down and shake him by the hand!"

"A guy from Aberfintry saved your aunt's life?" said Rory, wearying slightly that his day appeared to be gaining further complications.

"Yup, so the story goes. Apparently it was quite a big local incident. She was staying in a hotel and there was a fire ..."

Rory felt his throat tightening as he spoke. "Do you happen to know the name of the hotel?"

"Yeah ... it sounds a bit weird to me but apparently it's the family name."

"Hotel Grimm?" asked Rory, picturing a *Chronicle* headline about a fire from the framed pages beside Deirdre Dunbar's desk.

"That's the one. You know it?"

"Just a bit," said Rory weakly. "You can't miss it."

"Excellent! You can fill me in when I come over next week."

"You're coming over next week?" shouted Rory, picturing Finkleman arriving in the midst of *The Chronicle* kicking up a stink about the one place that he wanted to visit.

"Yeah, don't sound so happy about it, buddy!"

"Sorry, sorry, it's just there is quite a lot going on in the town at the moment."

"Perfect," said Finkleman. "I always like to visit a place when it's buzzing."

That's one word for it thought Rory. "Anyway," he said. "Do you know who the guy was that saved her life?"

"Some guy called … wait a minute. I have it here … Alistair McGroggan."

Rory looked blank. *McGroggan?* The name meant nothing to him. *Unless … Grog?* He tried to picture *The Chronicle* headline he had seen. *Inferno at Hotel Grimm. American tourist and staff member recovering in hospital.*

"Apparently he was the butler there," continued Finkleman. "Aunt Aggie took quite a shine to him from the sounds of things."

Rory tried to picture anyone finding Grog attractive and dismissed the thought immediately. "We can't be thinking about the same person then."

"He was a bit of a dancer apparently. My aunt would have loved that. Anyway the story goes that there was a fire in one of the rooms one night. One of the guests had left a candle burning. Aunt Aggie was next door to this, and the first she knew was this butler guy busting down the door and carrying her out. Real superhero stuff."

The painting of Grog that Rory had seen on Grimson's wall suddenly popped into his head. An upright man with a proud gaze and a look of fearlessness.

"Aunt Aggie needed a night or two in hospital, but she reckons she'd have been a gonner but for this character, McGroggan."

"Do you know what happened to him?" asked Rory, posing the question as innocently as possible.

"Apparently he did himself some damage in rescuing her, which she says she always felt guilty about."

"What sort of damage?" said Rory picturing the coughing, limping Grog.

"Pretty bad smoke inhalation and then just as he got her out of the building he fell and broke his ankle real bad. Do you think you can fix me up with a trip to this hotel when I come over?"

"Can we talk about it when you arrive?" said Rory.

"Sure thing, buddy. I'm looking forward to catching up with you. Need to talk to you about the next stage of the Zizz campaign too of course. Ever been to China?"

Rory just managed to stop himself groaning audibly before he put the phone down and sank his head firmly into his hands.

No ifs no buts
It has to shut
No ifs no buts
It has to shut

Chant of the Campaign for Closure

22. The campaign for closure

"This is outrageous." Rory slapped the copy of *The Chronicle* onto Grandad's cluttered coffee table. Old cups rattled in their saucers and a half-eaten biscuit catapulted on to the floor. The front page headline on the discarded paper lay taunting the room. "HOTEL MUST CLOSE NOW! Kidnap Cable Car Horror for Kids"

"Outrageous, but not very surprising," said Bonnie.

"Read it out to me," said Grandad.

"Do I have to read that rubbish?" asked Rory not really noticing that Grandad sounded weary today.

"Are you denying an old man his paper?" protested Grandad, trying to raise a joke and lifting his hands in a mock plea to Rory.

"Oh, give us a break. You turn that 'old man' routine on too often," snipped Rory reaching for the paper. Grandad put out a petted lip in jest, but said no more.

Rory began to read. "Whatever has gone on before, however patient the townspeople of Aberfintry have been, now is the time to rise up and demand the closure of the establishment that has blighted our beautiful town for over fifty years. Join the campaign now. Sign our petition. Cut out the poster page from your paper and put it in your window. Show your fellow citizens how you feel. Stand up and be counted."

Rory held up the page which readers were being encouraged to turn into their own window poster. It said "NO IFS NO BUTS. IT HAS TO SHUT." The words ran across a silhouette of Hotel Grimm, which had a big red cross scored through it. He carried on reading.

"Don't sit back and accept this any longer. Get up and join us. Show your commitment and come to the public demonstration at 11am on 22nd June at the Lachlan Stagg statue. There we will state our case and set out a timescale for action to end this period of shame in the life of our town and look forward together to a new beginning."

"Derek Goodman is like a one-man mission to shut that place down," said Bonnie.

"Aye well, we'll soon see if he *is* just a one-man mission, I suppose," said Grandad. "I think this'll bring a fair few people out of the woodwork."

"Well his usual sources have also contributed," said Rory reading on from the paper. "Bella Valentine, who has suffered at the hands of the hotel in the past commented, 'I'm just glad those kiddies are safe. That cable car contraption is an accident waiting to happen and the man who runs it ought to be turfed out of his bedroom in his garage.'" Rory then read out how Bella was inviting the Goodman twins to join her in setting up a survivors group for others like them who had experienced "a brush with death" at the hands of Hotel Grimm.

There was a downbeat mood in the room for the rest of the time that Rory and Bonnie were there. It seemed that recent events had had an impact on Grandad. He had lost some of his sparkle and appeared content just to sit and let Rory and Bonnie do most of the talking. The two of them found they were pretty much at a loss. They periodically picked up the paper and re-read it, as if hoping to find that the words had changed or that they had missed something positive.

Eventually realizing that Grandad was going to be happier just having a doze and not having to think about things that might bring up stories from the past, Rory and Bonnie left. With Grandad's earlier prediction still ringing in their ears, they headed up Boglehole Road wondering if people really were about to show their true colours. Their question was answered within the first two streets as they counted five windows sporting the cut-out posters.

"I thought it might have been worse," said Rory trying to be optimistic.

Bonnie was more gloomy. "Yeah, but that's only the start. The paper has only just come out. Some people won't have bought it yet. Others will but they won't have read it or had the time to track down their sticky tape".

"Got your copy yet?" The shout took them both by surprise. Max Fletcher was cycling past, and judging from the brightly-coloured bag he had on, he was in the middle of his paper round.

"You ought to be ashamed of yourself, putting these through people's doors," shouted Bonnie.

"Shut up, Worm," said Fletcher. "It's the end of the line for that place, and there's nothing you or Zizz Boy can do to stop it." His bike disappeared round the corner.

Bonnie and Rory agreed to check the same route the next day and sure enough the number of houses displaying posters had gone up to thirteen, with some shops joining in too. The day after that it was at twenty-nine. Rory began to feel very uncomfortable and decided to stop counting.

The worst thing was that even at school the campaign was taking shape, and it was no surprise that it was being led by Gordon and Gracie Goodman, who had now recovered from their cable car incident and were enjoying new-found celebrity status.

The first Rory knew about it was when he was approached by a second year he didn't know and asked if he wanted a "NO IFS NO BUTS" sticker for his schoolbag.

"Er, no thanks."

"You're the first one to say no," the girl said, as if this was big news in itself. As soon as he heard that, Rory knew that reports would soon get back that he wasn't joining in with the crowd. He thought about taking one just to save himself a lot of bother but knew he couldn't walk around sporting the slogan when he didn't agree with it. It only took a couple of days for word to get around and for the taunts to begin.

"Heh, Zizz Boy, I hear you're not joining in the campaign."

"He's best pals with the Grimms. I've heard he sits down to tea with them every now and then."

"Thinking of changing his name to Grimm Boy instead of Zizz Boy, isn't he?"

"Setting up camp on Scrab Hill is what I heard."

"Yeah, a tent for two for him and Bonnie."

"Zizz Boy and Bonnie are an item? That's *wheely* funny!"

Rory had hoped that the school might take a line on not allowing this sort of campaign to happen on the premises, but there was no such message coming out of the headteacher, Mrs Horne's office. In fact, some of the teachers had "NO IFS NO BUTS" car stickers much to Gracie and Gordon Goodman's delight. They were now holding lunchtime meetings in the playground with updates on the latest people to sign up to the campaign. There was much excitement one day as they were delighted to announce that Mrs Horne herself now had a car sticker. Shortly after this revelation, the Goodmans began the second phase of the campaign. Arriving at school and lost in thought about the demonstration which was now just ten days away, Rory had nearly walked past the people on the school gate holding clipboards before he realized what he had done.

"Oi! Sign this," said Max Fletcher.

"Sorry?" said Rory genuinely confused.

"It's a petition, Zizz Boy. We want the whole school to sign it." Marnie di Angelo sounded just as hostile.

"What's it for?" asked Rory stalling for time.

"Closing the hotel. Next stage of the "NO IFS NO BUTS" campaign," said Fletcher, sticking the clipboard an inch from Rory's face.

"I might sit this one out," said Rory ducking around it.

"Just sign it, Zizz Boy," said Marnie.

"I'd prefer not to," said Rory, "Thanks all the same." He headed away from the gate feeling eyes boring into the back of his head as he went.

"You'll regret that," shouted Marnie. "Whatever it is you're doing up there … it's a big mistake."

The last thing he heard was Fletcher saying, "I'll go and let Gordon and Gracie know."

Rory walked away, the heat creeping up the back of his neck. He was in a small and very silent minority and it didn't feel like a good place to be.

23. The Halfway House

Rory was keen to spend some time with Bonnie and Grandad trying to work out if there was any way to counter *The Chronicle's* campaign. At the same time he was no further forward with an answer to rebranding Hotel Grimm, with only a day to go until he was expected back there with solutions. Things seemed to have gone backwards instead of forwards. The three had all just settled down with mugs of tea in the living room at Boglehole Road when they heard the front door open.

"Yooo Hooo!" Rory's heart sank at the arrival and imminent interruption of his mother. To make matters worse, while Rory often felt a bit embarrassed by some of the outfits that his Mum wore, today she had taken things to a whole new level. Her shoes, skirt and top were perfectly split vertically into two halves. One side of her wore red and the other green. She had also extended the effect to her eyeshadow and Rory cringed to see that her hair sported two colours too, split perfectly down the middle of her new centre parting.

To make matters more bizarre, Momo was carrying a speed restriction road sign on a pole like giant lollipop. Half of the circular sign was missing creating a semi-circle. In the other hand she had a bag, which appeared to have been made out of recycled egg boxes and remnants of string woven together.

Rory was at a loss as to how his mother could put a positive spin on the ridiculous costume she had worn as she had walked down Boglehole Road.

"I'm *so* excited about my next exhibition," enthused Mrs McKenna having carefully put down her peculiar sign and bag.

"Oh no, not this one again," muttered Rory, rolling his eyes with a glance over at Grandad. He remembered managing to escape this explanation when he had bumped into his mum near *The Chronicle's* office.

Momo stopped suddenly on seeing Bonnie. "Hello," she said beaming. "I'm Momo … Rory's mum."

"This is Bonnie," Rory mumbled, cringing in embarrassment at his mum's general flamboyance. Bonnie smiled in greeting.

"So what's your exhibition about this time, dear?" asked Grandad, trying to sound as polite and interested as he could in whatever his daughter's latest plan was, as he winked at Rory.

"Half measures," said Momo with panache, beaming and looking at Grandad as if she had said enough for him to be as enthused as she was.

"You'll need to say just a wee bit more, to let me get the gist of it," said Grandad.

Momo began to move around the room, picking her way as best she could between coffee table and settee and squeezing past Bonnie. "Half Measures," she announced again with arms raised, her eyes widening with excitement as she visualized what this exhibition would consist of. "This won't just be a collection of pieces of art, this will be a movement in society." Grandad looked at Rory and pretended to fall asleep. Momo failed to notice. "What if we, each one of us here in this room, or every person in Aberfintry, or in Scotland, or in the UK, or in Europe, or in the world or …"

"Yes, Mum," said Rory. "We get the drift. What if a lot of people what …?"

"I was coming to that," said Momo. "What if all of us only had, used, bought or said half as much as we normally do?"

Momo looked at Rory, Grandad and Bonnie, expecting them to be already on board her rapidly speeding train of thought. She was unfazed by the blank looks that met her and carried on. "Imagine if we went half the speed of normal, ate half as much as normal, said half as much as normal, bought half as much as normal, threw away half as much as normal … if we thought a bit more, held back a bit more, considered not throwing our whole weight around any more. If things were in half measures my question to you is … would we be half the people we are, or twice the people we are? Let's stop halfway and become more."

She left the last sentence hanging in the air, her arms outstretched. Rory couldn't help thinking that the world would be a better place if his Mum held only half of the exhibitions that she did. Grandad, however, seemed a bit more taken with Momo's idea.

"Aye, you have a point," he said. "Everything is too fast-paced these days, and people don't really care what they say or what they use some of the time."

"It sort of fits with people starting to recycle more," said Bonnie.

"Exactly, dear," said Momo. "If people just held back a bit in every aspect of life, the world would be a different place. We would all look at things differently. Can't you see? This could be the start of something really big. A campaign … a movement … we all sign up to Stop Halfway?" She held out a hand like a traffic policeman signalling "stop."

"Well it's a good idea, Morag. Mind you, I'm not sure how you turn a good idea into a movement," said Grandad.

Bonnie chirped up. "People sometimes just need an example and they get the idea that life could be different. Look at *The Chronicle's* campaign. It's like people were just waiting for someone to take the lead. Give them a different idea and they might go off in a new direction."

The conversation carried on but Rory wasn't fully aware of what Bonnie, Grandad or his Mum were saying any more. A strange tingly feeling had gripped the back of his neck and his mouth had gone dry. Ideas seemed to be connecting into place in his head in such a way that he could almost hear them clicking as they did so.

"The telescope," said Rory. He felt so peculiar and distracted that his voice sounded detached as he spoke. He shook his head to clear it and jumped up. Momo, Grandad and Bonnie looked at him in surprise.

"I need the telescope," said Rory. "I need the telescope." He pushed his way over to the window.

"All right, all right, calm down," said Bonnie

as he bumped the coffee table sending a pile of magazines sliding to the floor. The room fell silent as Rory scanned and focused. Three people behind him looked at each other and shrugged. "Is he all right?" whispered Momo.

"Just give the lad a wee minute," said Grandad.

"There's the solution," said Rory in a quiet voice. "That's it."

"What is? What can you see?" said Bonnie.

Rory turned back to face them all. "Mum, your exhibition sounds fantastic. Inspirational in fact." Momo looked confused and flattered that her son had decided to pay her a few compliments. Uncertain what she had done or what she ought to do now, she began to play with her beads.

"Well, I don't know what to say. It's early days for this idea, but I do always try to do things that have an impact on people."

"You have this time. Believe me," said Rory with determined sincerity. Grandad grumbled something about Rory changing his tune.

Bonnie got exasperated. "Come on, Mr Genius. I seem to remember that the last time you declared that you'd cracked it, you were the only one who agreed with yourself, *and* you went on to be wrong. What's the great idea this time?"

"Rebranding Hotel Grimm," said Rory in a quiet voice. "That was the challenge and this is the answer. It's not about trying to repackage what the hotel is. Finkleman is right. You can't sell the unsellable. Do you know, I'm not even sure Granville Grimm or Grog for that matter wants it to be a hotel anyway. The answer is about creating something different altogether. A fresh start. A chance to do things differently. Some new place that's neither the hotel nor the town. A place that people do want. A halfway house."

"Well if you're looking out of the window, then halfway is in the middle of nowhere, on Scrab Hill," pointed out Bonnie.

"Exactly. The Halfway House," said Rory as if it meant something.

"What are you talking about, Rory?" said Bonnie. "What halfway house?"

"Why not make it that people go halfway up the hill to do business with the Grimms, rather than going *all* the way to the hotel?"

Bonnie gave Rory a look that suggested that he had gone completely mad. "You can't use a hotel without going into it. How can you go halfway to a hotel?"

"Not to a hotel," replied Rory. "To the pavilion on the ledge. Turn it into a café with the best view in the area, where people can't help but see things differently. That would be the unique selling point of the place for anyone who lives in the town … the fact that it's not in the town."

"You're forgetting something," said Bonnie. "You talk about a café, but the pavilion is a wreck according to your description and the hotel is a cesspit. Surely no one wants food that comes out of those places?"

"There's a lot to do to the place, but the food is no problem. Ramsay Sandilands will sort that out. He'll cook to save them all!"

"The rat collector as the cook?" spluttered

Bonnie. "Now that is a marketing challenge. Come and eat at our café ... we're giving away free diseases as a special offer!"

"You'll have to trust me on this one. It will work," said Rory calmly, picturing Ramsay Sandilands' scrupulously clean kitchen.

"One problem you have is that you're going to need some pretty fit customers if you want them to climb a hill like that to get a cup of coffee and a bun," said Grandad. "Surely that's the project dead in the water before you've even begun. I'll not be likely to pop in for a wee cuppa."

"That's where you're wrong, Grandad," replied Rory with a knowing smile. "I expect to see you up there. You're forgetting something. We've got a cable car that stops just up from the ledge. It's primed and ready to go, with an operator who has been waiting for years for some passengers."

Grandad nodded slowly. "Aye, right enough, Stobo would have kept that in good order. But will anyone dare go near him?"

"Your Grandad's right," said Bonnie. "It's all very well having a new place to go to and transport to take you there. But if the name Grimm has anything to do with it, then it's doomed to failure from the start." Rory shook his head.

"Oh come on, Rory," said Bonnie. "You've counted the posters in the houses around here. You don't think they are suddenly going to be ripped down just because you offer people the chance of a ride to get a scone and a cappuccino?"

"Trust me. This *is* the answer," said Rory.

"That's what you said the last time you got

enthusiastic," said Bonnie. Rory didn't reply, and tried not to let Bonnie's comment unsettle him. He knew he couldn't afford to be wrong twice, for his sake or the Grimms.

"I'd go up there," said Momo who had been listening quietly until now. She was in a state of shock that her exhibition plans had already caused so much discussion. "I might get even more inspiration from a new vantage point."

Grandad's forehead crinkled up in concern. "I'm not sure we can cope with too many life-changing movements. Maybe you'd better stay down here in the town!"

A short time later as they left Grandad's house, and before they had even reached the end of his front path, Rory noticed a "NO IFS NO BUTS" poster in the window of the next-door house. Although he thought that his latest idea was a strong one, he couldn't help but think that someone or something else was going to be needed to push it through. With a week to go to the demonstration, he hadn't even told Granville Grimm of this latest proposal, while the pavilion that was at the heart of the solution he proposed was a complete wreck.

But his biggest problem remained the small matter of the typical Aberfintry resident's refusal to go up Scrab Hill. What were the chances of their opinions being changed by the combined voices of a falsely-lauded marketing expert, his bookish friend, housebound grandfather and a wacky artist?

"It's fizzy, it's light, Zizz has got it right"

Winner of the Most Memorable Advertising Slogan of the Year

24. Confession

Rory felt his hand being enveloped and pumped up and down by a giant paw-like grasp.

"Man, it's good to see you again, Rory! I know it sounds corny, but you are growing fast!"

So are you, thought Rory who had arranged to meet the somewhat-larger-than-before, Mr Finkleman at the Art Gallery Café for old times sake.

"It sure is funny being back here again," Finkleman said, looking round the sunny terrace. "What a chance meeting that was. I've often thought it was meant to be."

Rory smiled a weak smile of agreement. As he looked out at the sculptures in the garden he pictured the girl skipping past and singing. Maybe she would turn up today just to complete the reunion.

"So what's been happening, buddy? I couldn't help noticing all of these "No Ifs No Buts" posters around the town. What's going on? Something about a big demonstration next weekend?"

Rory was lost for words. So much had happened in the last three weeks that he couldn't think where to start.

"Well to be honest, it's all about the hotel you have an interest in," said Rory.

"Yeah, I need to get up there and do what Aunt Aggie wanted me to," said Finkleman. "You'll need to point me in the right direction."

Rory stuck out an arm and pointed to Scrab Hill and Hotel Grimm.

"Wow, that place?" said Finkleman looking at its dark forbidding shape. "Aunt Aggie always did live life on the edge!"

"Well, I can take you up there and introduce you," said Rory. "I've sent a message ahead to explain that you're coming. So you'll hopefully get a decent welcome." His fear was that Grog would be as rude to the nephew of the woman he had saved in the fire, as he had been to Rory on his first visit there. He had sent a note to Grog, and a lengthy one to Grimson too, courtesy of Stobo and the cable car, to try and ensure that Finkleman wouldn't turn tail and run as soon as the door creaked open.

"I can fill you in on what's been happening on the way up. I need to pitch an idea to them and have a meeting there this afternoon."

"Excellent," said Finkleman. "No time like the present, and good to hear you are back in business again. Ideas from the Zizz Boy are sure to be worth making an appointment for."

By the time they got to the ledge, Rory had covered as much of the background story as he could.

Finkleman didn't say much. This was partly because he was puffing and bright red from the exertion of climbing the hill, "Man, I am out of shape," he said, but also because he was taking in everything that Rory was saying. He would alternately nod, shake his head or whistle in wonder at the stories Rory was telling.

At the ledge they finally stopped for air. Rory felt like he had offloaded much of what had been swilling around in his head in recent times. The view was as good as ever and Finkleman was not disappointed. "Wow, Rory, I see what you're thinking. This is some vantage point." He moved over to the edge and breathed in deeply. "I gotta get out of the city for a while. Look at me," he said patting his large stomach. "I'm carrying a few too many pounds. Do you know I could use a break. The last eighteen months have been super-busy."

Finkleman turned back to Rory. "See buddy, this place is working for me already!" He looked beyond Rory to the pavilion. "Hey, check that out! Is that what you reckon could be the Halfway House? What a place!" He walked towards it. "Seven days to fix it up you say? Well we've fitted out some of the new Zizz café bars in that sort of time just to get them open, but this is quite a challenge."

"The main problem is that there is no local builder who will touch this place," said Rory.

"Shame," said Finkleman, "It reminds me of stuff I used to do when I had the time. Building things. I renovated a few houses in my younger days. I loved all that stuff. I'm too used to sitting down and pushing a pen these days."

"We should probably go," said Rory, getting depressed. The more he thought about it, the more his solution was sounding quite unfeasible, given the tight timescale.

"Sure thing. At least I have my breath back now," said Finkleman. "Do you know, Rory, I'm touched by the story of your Grandad. That must have been so difficult for him living with secrets like that for so long. I'm sure he must feel like a new man having had the chance to talk to you this week."

Rory nodded. Looking down on the town, he could just make out Boglehole Road and the workshop at the bottom of the garden. A few streets away, the Art Gallery Café with its little outdoor area could also be seen. It struck Rory that he was with Finkleman, talking about the value of honesty and the pain of secrets in a place where everything looked different.

"There's one other thing I ought to tell you, but this one is a bit difficult to explain," said Rory continuing to look down on Aberfintry. Knowing that he was almost at a point of no return, he just couldn't look Finkleman in the eye.

"Well, Rory," said Finkleman, "you fire away and I'll see if I can make sense of it."

"Er ... yes it's one of those things," continued Rory, his mouth beginning to dry up. "... or rather it's a situation where what everyone thinks is the real story, isn't actually the case and it's quite hard explaining just what the truth actually is."

"Okay, well you have a go and we'll see where we get to," said Finkleman, still cheery and encouraging.

Why oh why didn't I just say this in the first place at the Art Gallery Café, thought Rory to himself. "It's just knowing quite where to start," he said.

"Well I always find the beginning a useful enough place to get going from," said Finkleman.

Rory instinctively checked the distance to get back to the path in case Finkleman's reaction meant that he needed to make a sharp getaway. There was a long pause. Rory could no longer think of anything to say to stall the inevitable.

"Come on Rory. I'm all ears," said Finkleman. "Whatever it is, just spit it out."

"It's about the Zizz slogan," blurted out Rory.

"Ah ... your miracle moment of genius," said Finkleman grandly.

"Well, you see, that's just it," said Rory squirming inside and now feeling very hot under the collar. "That was one miracle that is actually very easy to explain."

"You're speaking in code here, Rory. Just let me know what you want to say. The truth can't hurt," said Finkleman with a grin and spreading his arms.

"The truth is ... the Zizz slogan wasn't mine."

There was silence from Finkleman this time, raising Rory's anxiety levels still further. Rory was finding it hard to look at the big American but sneaked a peak. His eyes had narrowed and his mouth seemed to have tightened. Rory could almost imagine his brain in overdrive, processing just what he was hearing. "This is what we would call in the trade 'an interesting development,' Rory," drawled Finkleman. "I seem to remember, when I asked how you would describe Zizz all those months ago, that's what you came out with."

"I know, but I had just heard someone else say it." Rory explained the real situation. It sounded cheap and nasty. Finkleman raised his eyebrows and then to Rory's surprise seemed to carry on as normal.

"Yeah, but when I asked how you would describe Zizz, that's what you said and that for me was the right answer."

"Yeah, but I used someone else's idea," said Rory, aware that he had gone bright red on the outside and had a hollow feeling inside.

"Well, Rory, they sure haven't been in touch with me to make a claim about it. The way I see it is … you gave me the right answer when I asked you a question, and that answer has brought our company phenomenal success. Okay your creative qualities perhaps aren't as strong as I thought, and maybe that award was pushing it a bit, but hey, you gave us the idea we needed, and look where Zizz Cola is now. Sometimes in this job it's just about timing."

"So you don't mind?" said Rory finally bringing himself to look Finkleman fully in the eye.

"Mind? Mind that I manage the number one soft drinks company in the world? I'm not sure what your problem is really, Rory," said Finkleman. "Listen, where do you think any idea comes from in the first place? Some combination of things people have seen before … some connection they make between things. Everyone gets their ideas from something or someone if you trace them back. Okay you could have told me about this before. We could even have tried to find whoever had said this line originally. But this isn't an unusual situation. There is nothing new under the sun. The clever thing is to put ideas together with the situation that needs them. Now that's what you did. Don't you worry, buddy. You get to keep the plaque and all those free cans of Zizz."

"I wasn't really bothered about those," said Rory mumbling and finding it hard to believe that what had been preying on his mind for so long had just been dismissed out of hand.

"Well Mr Marketing Genius ... I'm not going to strip you of your title, especially given the idea that you have come up with here. Now if you pitch this proposal up at the hotel just now and turn this place around," Finkleman gestured around the ledge, "that will *really* be marketing genius. You would have sorted out a decades-old image problem in one fell swoop, increased a company's profits, not to mention the community benefits of the project. Buddy, you would be in line for some kind of award!"

Finkleman saw the pained expression on Rory's face at the thought of it, and his roar of laughter echoed over the ledge and beyond.

"That is some piece of work," said Finkleman. He stood beside Rory looking down on the fallen statue of the wolf.

"So you really think that all the bad stuff has just been coincidence then?" said Finkleman. "This so-called curse was just hot air?"

"Well, as time has gone on it just seems that everything has an explanation," said Rory thinking it all through. The hotel no longer scared him. Granville Grimm was now someone he felt sorry for rather than afraid of. The mural was not painting itself. He had found out about good people like Grimson and Gwendolen Grimm. Stobo was not the ogre that most believed, and it seemed that Grog was a surprise package. Far from being a death trap, the cable car brought a whole new view to Scrab Hill. Rory was even trying to see rats in a new light courtesy of Ramsay Sandilands. Meanwhile, much of how the town viewed the hotel seemed to have been influenced by Derek Goodman, and he had his own personal reasons for that. Bella Valentine's story had played a part too, and as Rory remembered her, he realized that there was one unanswered question about the hotel.

"There is one thing that's not been explained yet," said Rory as they approached the enormous front door. "I might just check it out while we're here."

"Hi," said Rory as the door was opened. The welcome and response was remarkably different from his first visit.

"Good afternoon," croaked Grog holding the door open. "Mr McKenna for Mr Grimm?"

"That's right but I'm very early, so I was going to pop up and see Grimson first," said Rory. "I think I can find my own way, if that's okay?"

"As you wish," said Grog. "And you must be Ms Finkleman's nephew."

"I am indeed and I have strict instructions to shake you very firmly by the hand, Mr McGroggan. It is a pleasure and an honour to meet you."

Grog looked flattered. "Well, any relative of Ms Finkleman is very welcome at the hotel. I remember her visit with great affection, even though it ended under difficult circumstances." Grog stifled a cough. "Please do come in."

Rory watched Finkleman trying to adjust his eyes to the gloom. The burly American looked across at Rory as if to say "I see what you mean."

"Our chef has prepared some afternoon tea if you would care to come through here," said Grog.

"Sure glad you briefed me about this, Rory," whispered Finkleman as he followed Grog.

Rory took his leave and headed upstairs intent on ruling out the last big question mark over Hotel Grimm. Just why was Corridor Five off limits?

If you want to stay alive
Stay well clear of Corridor Five
It's there you'll find a beast resides
All set to dine on your insides

Winning entry for the Bella Valentine
Hallowe'en Poetry Competition

25. Corridor Five

Having survived two trips to Hotel Grimm already, Rory no longer believed that sudden death awaited him there; not even in Corridor Five. If he could disprove Bella Valentine's story that there was some kind of beast there, then people's fears about the hotel might diminish and the idea of the Halfway House would stand more of a chance of at least being heard. Until that happened she would always say: "That place is evil and was nearly the death of me."

As he headed upstairs, Rory felt more confident in the gloom of the hotel now, being a bit clearer on his sense of direction around the building. He also felt more confident as he still had Bonnie's giant torch with him. It had been in his backpack since he had used it to identify Grimson, and now it helped to locate the corridor numbers. Within a couple of minutes he was standing at the sign for Corridor Five, the beam of the torch picking out the number high on the wall.

Rory's confidence in his hunch that there was some explanation behind Corridor Five's mystery began to shake a little at the sight of the sign. To avoid getting scared, he had been telling himself that the noise that had begun so suddenly when he was here with Grog would be about to start again. "Anytime now," he said to himself, "it's going to happen anytime now. Not a problem. Not a problem at all. Just a loud noise. All perfectly normal ..."

In front of him was a short section of hallway, a right-hand corner and then Corridor Five would begin properly. It was as he moved towards the corner that his prediction proved to be correct.

BANG CLATTER BANG CLATTER BANG CLATTER

"Told you, told you, told you," he said to himself. Rory was all too aware that even though he had prepared himself for this, his heart was already starting to thump much faster than normal. The thought that Bella Valentine might not have exaggerated and that a spitting, clanking, chomping beast intent on devouring him in one gulp might be round the corner, suddenly assaulted Rory's nerves.

"There's no such thing, there's no such thing ... there's a simple explanation, there's a simple explanation," Rory told himself as firmly as he could, as he took another pace forward.

BANG CLATTER HISS BANG CLATTER HISS BANG CLATTER HISS

Rory shuddered. The power of positive thinking was struggling to compete with the increasing noise. He was very aware he didn't want to provoke the beast any more and turned off the torch for fear that the light might make the creature even more ferocious.

BANG CLATTER HISS WHEEZE BANG CLATTER HISS WHEEZE BANG CLATTER

Rory was now standing at the corner. Going around it would take him fully into Corridor Five and face to face with the beast of Hotel Grimm.

BANG CLATTER HISS WHEEZE CRASH MOAN BANG CLATTER HISS WHEEZE CRASH MOAN BANG CLATTER

The noises were now pounding in his ears. Wincing and holding his breath he rounded the corner. The noise in the darkness was too much for him. Rory reached for the light switch on the wall and flicked it down but nothing happened. The click seemed to ignite something further in the beast and the volume increased.

BANG CLATTER HISS WHEEZE CRASH MOAN ROAR BANG CLATTER HISS WHEEZE CRASH MOAN ROAR BANG CLATTER

Alarm bells began to sound in his head. Bella Valentine was right! He had badly misjudged Corridor Five. He was about to become front page news in *The Chronicle* for all the wrong reasons. Finkleman would tell how he found only bits of the Zizz Boy left.

And then he saw it. Out of the deep darkness at the end of the corridor lurched an immense misshapen figure. Rory could make out little detail but there was no doubt Bella Valentine's story was coming to life in front of his eyes and was frighteningly accurate. "Hold your nerve! Hold your nerve!" he told himself as the creature advanced.

BANG CLATTER HISS WHEEZE CRASH MOAN ROAR BANG CLATTER HISS WHEEZE CRASH MOAN ROAR BANG CLATTER

The cacophony grew louder and louder and closer and closer. He could virtually feel the beat of the noise on his skin. The beast was now roaring wildly, swaying from side to side and moving slowly towards him. Rory's hands shook uncontrollably and he dropped the torch. Falling to his knees he scrabbled desperately to find it. He flinched as a misty spray settled on his brow. It could only be fine spittle from a roaring mouth above him and Rory panicked that it might burn his skin like acid. The noise was now deafening as it seemed that whatever it was standing right above him. Rory smelt acrid smoke from the monster's lungs and he screamed as his hand struck teeth, only to realize that he had brushed the head of a tiger-skin rug on the corridor floor. In one move he grabbed the rug with both hands and threw it upwards with all his strength. The roaring momentarily became more muffled. Rory scrabbled for the torch, his hand finally connecting with it. He dived to the side of the corridor, flicked the switch and shone the bright light straight at the beast.

The creature was tottering around fighting to get the tiger skin off its head and in doing so it walked straight into a doorpost. "Ouch!" it said in a muffled, metallic but remarkably human-sounding way. Flailing its arms, the tiger-skin rug fell away and Rory was confused to see some sort of apparatus for a head. He held his torch arm as stiff and steady as he could, pointing the light as if he were pumping bullets from a gun. Whatever it was had thrown an arm in front of its face. For all the sound, smell and spray it looked like a normal arm on a normal person, albeit with a few things attached.

If Rory was taken aback to hear the creature say "ouch" he was even more surprised when it said: "Listen you couldn't switch that light off, could you? It's really awfully bright."

Stunned at the sound, Rory moved the beam to one side trying to work out how this roaring monster could have such a polite voice. The creature lowered its arm and Rory could now see that the apparatus he had seen was an old army gas mask topped by what looked like a shower head dripping the last of its spray. A set of tubes linked it to a water container carried on the creature's back. Eyes flickered behind the goggles. Anything remotely scary had vanished as the light revealed a rather ridiculous home-made costume. As the creature took a couple of paces to the side, the wheezing breathing noise began again. Tubes connected from a set of bellows between its legs ran up forcing air through the mouthpiece of the gas mask, creating the heavy rasping breathing sound. Cymbals were strapped to its elbows and body, so that simple movements created a clashing sound. A wisp of pungent smoke could now be seen coming from a canister strapped to a man's left arm.

"I thought you were some kind of fire-breathing monster," said Rory, sitting back against the wall, an air of relief in his voice.

"That's what you were supposed to think," said the man's muffled voice. "That's what people always think if they get this far. They don't usually have as good a torch as that, or if they do, then they don't stand around long enough to use it."

"Did you make all of that?" asked Rory looking at the bizarre outfit.

"All my own work," said the voice as the figure worked at loosening the gas mask straps and lifting the headpiece off. Rory looked closely at the man behind the beast. He had a patchily whiskered chin and crazy white hair sticking up in clumps between where the straps of his gas mask had been. For some reason the man had a paperclip attached to his chin and as Rory studied him further, he noticed that the top of his left ear was missing.

With a start, Rory realized that he was facing a dead man.

"I know who you are," said Rory.

"What's that, dear boy?" The man's eyes flitted around momentarily as if weighing up his options to escape or make up a story.

"Lachlan Stagg," said Rory.

The man looked startled as if it was some time since he had heard his name being spoken.

"You are Lachlan Stagg," continued Rory in an unbelieving voice. "Your ear is missing. *You* were missing. You're supposed to be dead, but you've been here all along, haven't you? HAVEN'T YOU?"

"Er ... well, I suppose I have," said the man scratching his head in a slightly embarrassed manner.

"What have you been doing here?" said Rory.

"Well, I ... um ... I ... er ... I live here," replied Lachlan Stagg, looking away and struggling to meet Rory's hard stare. "For the moment at least," he added.

"What do you mean you live here?" said Rory. "How come? Why? People think you're dead? What are you doing here?"

"Well I've been trying to get the elusive last four."

"Last four what?" said Rory confused.

"Records, young man. World records," said Stagg, shaking himself out of the straps that kept all of the apparatus on his arms and back.

"I don't understand," said Rory. "What has disappearing got to do with world records?"

"Well that is precisely it. When I was doing research around here for the gargoyles book I thought to myself 'you could have some fun hiding in here.' I checked the record for the person who had hidden for the longest time and until you came along I only had another 125 days to go to gain the record! You've rather trodden on my patch, dear boy!" said Stagg. "All that effort gone to waste. I was rather looking forward to reappearing and claiming the title. It's really a bit of a poor show after all this time. Jolly inconvenient of you to turn up and be so persistent."

"I thought you said you needed four records, not just one," said Rory trying to process the fact that the town's local celebrity who was missing presumed dead, had been at the root of the belief that the hotel housed a monstrous beast.

"I do. So in the time I've been hiding I've concentrated on gaining the other ones that I needed. I've taught myself Spanish … or should I say 'Me he enseñado a mí mismo el castellano' to add to my qualifications. After much work up and down this corridor I can stay on a unicycle for six hours and thirty-one minutes and I have grown this …" With great care, Stagg detached the paperclip from his chin and inch by inch began to uncurl the most enormous chin hair that Rory had ever seen.

By the time he had finished it curled down to his waist.

"I've had a lot of peace and quiet to work on them all. No one really dares to come up here since I developed my er … shall we say diversionary tactics."

"No wonder," said Rory. "They think they're going to be attacked. Bella Valentine has been dining out on this story for two years. Wait until it's revealed that it was some bellows, a gas mask and a shower head! How have you managed to survive for so long?"

"Well pretty much everything I need is here … bathroom at the end of the corridor, a stairway that takes you up to the north-east turret so I can get fresh air. And I have some access to other parts of the building," said Stagg. "I'll show you." Walking over to a small door at the far corner of the corridor, Stagg disappeared inside. "Come and have a look," he shouted. Rory faltered. A few minutes ago he had been facing the beast of Corridor Five and now he was entering a dark unknown space with the man behind it all and nobody knew he was here. He also realized that if Lachlan Stagg did away with him, then he could still claim that he had remained hidden and wait another hundred or so days before reappearing. Rory decided that there was something about Lachlan Stagg that seemed as though he could cope with being found and that he would find another record to break.

"Here goes," said Rory heading through the door and down a tiny tight spiral staircase. Immediately it seemed familiar from his tour with Grog. "This way," came Stagg's voice from below. There was already a hint of light in the distance and Rory emerged into a familiar space as he stepped through a door in the wall lined with books. They were in the library.

"You're the poltergeist!"

"I beg your pardon?" said Stagg.

"Bella Valentine reckoned that there was a poltergeist in here because the books kept moving, but it was you."

"I've read most of the contents of this room. Yes I suspect I haven't always put things back in the right place," he said with a vague wave of his hand.

"What have you done for food?" asked Rory. "You don't look like you've been starving yourself."

"Ah … well … that is one area I was going to have to negotiate with the world record authorities …"

"Why?" asked Rory. "Aren't you supposed to eat if you are trying to get the 'hiding for the longest time' record?"

"No … you see … I have had a little help," said Stagg looking slightly embarrassed.

"Some help?" said Rory. "You mean someone else knows that Lachlan Stagg is still alive?"

Rory had a fleeting thought that his Grandad had kept yet another secret from him, but dismissed it. Not even the old man could pull that one off. Then he realized. Food. Joint world records for pancake making.

"Ramsay Sandilands," he said.

"He has kept me rather too well fed, I think," said Stagg patting his tummy. "I've tried to work it off on the unicycle but I've never been able to go very far unfortunately."

"Ramsay did sound quite sure that there would be an end to the hotel's troubles," said Rory remembering their conversation in the kitchen.

"This has been the other reason for me staying here, you see," said Stagg. "Ramsay thought that this episode might put the hotel on the map. He said to me that the hotel needed a big story. A positive story. People might want to come to the place where a world record was set. They might even want to see, or stay in Corridor Five where someone remained hidden for so long. I was happy to help. I think this place is fascinating. Always have done since I wrote the book about it. In the long term I thought this might help Granville Grimm out, even though he is in the dark about it all at the moment."

Having recently tried to crack the impossible problem of finding a way to sell the idea of staying in the hotel, Rory could see some logic in their madcap scheme, but he also knew that a solution was now needed quicker than Ramsay Sandilands' plan could provide.

"You may not know, but things have moved on a bit down in the town," said Rory. "I'm afraid it's going to take a bit more than a world record to get people up here. You ought to see this." He rummaged in his backpack and handed over his copy of *The Chronicle* with its "HOTEL MUST CLOSE NOW" headline to Lachlan Stagg. Reaching into the breast pocket of his tweed jacket, Stagg pulled out a pair of half-moon glasses to read. As he did so his eyes misted over and his brow furrowed. He cleared his throat in an awkward manner. "Oh dear. This is *not* good."

"Half the town has these posters up," said Rory.

"Dear me, dear me," said Stagg. "Is this really where things have got to? This is not right. Not right at all."

He flicked through the paper. Rory knew its contents inside out and knew they didn't get any better.

"I fear our efforts have not helped after all," said Stagg. "I knew this would come to an end at some point … and now seems to be the time." He folded the paper and handed it back to Rory. "Thank you for coming today. I described it as an inconvenience upstairs but it is far from it. You were very brave and it was the right thing to do. I think I should make some immediate arrangements to reappear!"

"That will certainly rock the boat of Derek Goodman's campaign," said Rory. He was thoughtful for a moment and then realized that this was the answer. He had known that something or someone was needed to promote the idea of the Halfway House. Lachlan Stagg was just the man.

"This could just be perfect … yes, yes, yes … you would be perfect!" exclaimed Rory. "This is just what we need! If you can tell people that the hotel isn't what they think it is, then that will work! They'll trust you!"

"I'm not sure about that after this little escapade," said Stagg, returning his glasses to his pocket.

"But they love you," said Rory. "There's a big statue to you in the middle of the town!"

"Yes, Ramsay told me that. But now they're going to find out that I've not exactly been honest with them," said Stagg. "I think I may have turned myself from the good guy into the bad guy. I suspect that rather changes the way they view my opinion."

"I see your point," said Rory, thinking it through. "But I think that it's a gamble that we'll just have to take. You're the best chance we have."

"Well then. I must pack my bag and come downhill to stand up and be counted. One can't go on living a lie for ever."

"Well you can get some practice in coming clean here before you start down in the town," said Rory.

"I'm sorry, dear boy?" said Lachlan Stagg looking a bit vague.

"Well," said Rory, "I think you owe Granville Grimm an explanation don't you?"

"Yes, yes of course. You are quite right, quite right," said Stagg fingering his brow and looking slightly troubled. "I suppose I do rather have some apologising to do to my landlord of the last few years."

Rory looked at his watch and gulped. He was supposed to be in a meeting with Granville Grimm in about thirty seconds. It was a sign of how things had changed that he didn't expect to be decapitated for turning up late. Still, arriving with a man who had remained hidden in the building for years, and who had helped to keep people away from it, might just put serious bodily harm back on the agenda. Who knew what Granville Grimm might do when faced with the truth about Lachlan Stagg?

26. The hit squad

At least Rory had some company. Harvey Finkleman was there. Having survived his afternoon tea experience he said he couldn't wait to hear Rory pitch the idea of the Halfway House. Before Granville Grimm arrived for the meeting, Rory only had time to whisper to him that there had been a rather major development since they had arrived in the hotel. It took less than ten minutes to describe the idea of the Halfway House to Granville Grimm, who nodded thoughtfully throughout and commented that the pavilion had always been a favourite place of his.

Rory then took the bull by the horns and started the explanation about what had been going on in Corridor Five, highlighting that it had happened with the hotel's long-term interests at heart. He then introduced a rather embarrassed looking Lachlan Stagg who had been waiting outside in the hall like a naughty schoolboy in line to see the headmaster. The tweed-suited eccentric took over with a very long, very eloquent and very sincere apology. Finkleman shook his head slowly. "Well I'll be ..." he said. "That is one heck of a story."

Granville Grimm was seated in his customary position at the far end of the long table considering every word with an impassive expression. As Stagg finished, there was a long pause. Rory looked fearfully at the hulking hotel owner. He appeared to have been frozen by the news he had just been told. What was of most concern was that Granville Grimm had closed his eyes and his breathing seemed to be picking up pace. Rory felt beads of sweat begin to form. As he watched, Grimm's forehead knitted into a deep frown and his body began to twitch with his shoulders jerking up and down. Rory decided in a stomach-lurching instant that he was in deep trouble. Granville Grimm raised a bony finger and pointed. Rory flinched, knowing now for sure there really was evil at the heart of this man. He braced himself for a puff of smoke and a curse on him and Lachlan Stagg for the rest of their lives. Expecting the spell to strike at any moment he shut his eyes tight. Nothing happened. Rory risked a peek towards Granville Grimm. The man was now shaking his head very slowly and then as if in some weird rhythm his shoulders began moving in time too. The speed picked up, faster and faster until his whole frame was juddering. Wide-eyed, Rory continued to watch and then the noise began. A slow, huffing, wheezing noise at first as if Granville Grimm was struggling for air and then.

"WAHAHAHAHAHAHAHAHAHA!"

Granville Grimm's head snapped back, his mouth gaping open and his whole body shuddering as he roared with laughter. The sound went on and on and on. Every ten seconds his head would slump to his chest just long enough to suck in a huge gulp of air and then he was off again.

"WAHAHAHAHAHAHAHAHAHA!"

After the fifth time, Rory's fear had long since dissolved and he was beginning to chuckle himself at the sight of the supposedly sinister hotel owner so uncontrollably consumed by laughter that tears were pouring down his face.

Rory looked to one side to see Lachlan Stagg's shoulders beginning to quiver too. He still looked a bit embarrassed to be at the root of this outburst, but equally he couldn't help laughing at the helpless man at the other end of the table. As the noise continued, Rory became aware of the other people in the room.

Mr Finkleman was chuckling deeply. The effect of his shoulders and big belly quivering in accompaniment to his laughter made him seem even rounder. Standing to one side of the door, Grog shuffled his feet nervously as if not quite sure what to do next, but within another minute, he too began to be taken over by the roaring laughter of his master, his mouth splitting back and up his cheeks to form a crocodile smile and the start of a snickering laugh, interspersed with a cough or two. There was a movement off to Rory's left side. It was Grimson.

Never one to let things faze him too much, Grimson was silent amidst the cacophony of laughter, but even he sported a huge broad grin as he watched his father in convulsions at the far end of the table. It seemed as though they were witnessing years of weariness and sad news falling away from the hotel owner, like he was shedding layers of unwanted skin.

Rory felt that, finally, he understood Granville Grimm. Lachlan Stagg had effectively helped to put the brakes on any potential business success and had unwittingly contributed to the hotel owner's troubles, yet when Grimm eventually regained his composure, he simply sat back, his face now lighter and more animated than Rory had seen before, and was thoroughly decent about the whole thing.

"There have been many factors at play here and you, Lachlan, are only one of them. I appreciate that in the long term you had my interests at heart, and in some strange way you have helped to bring us to this point. It would seem that you may now be perfectly positioned to help us move on. I do not accept your apology … because I do not believe you have one to give."

With Granville Grimm firmly on side, Rory decided that he had the perfect moment to reveal the full extent of his proposal. Describing the campaign being waged by Derek Goodman, Rory suggested that it could be thwarted by attempting to transform the pavilion and open The Halfway House in seven days.

Nobody spoke as worried glances were exchanged at the short timescale.

"Well, as you know, I love a challenge," said Lachlan Stagg, breaking the silence. "I would regard it as an honour and a duty to lead this task. Presumably you need joinery and glazing skills at the very least. They are two of the qualifications I have achieved in the past, and I'd be delighted to put them to good use."

"Gentlemen, I wonder if I, too, can offer my services?" It was Finkleman who spoke. "These are skills that I also have, and I think a working holiday is just what I need at the moment. I'll need to make a few calls to get out of some meetings, but if you'll have me I shall be glad to join you for this challenge."

As Grog stepped forward, Rory remembered Grimson's opinion of the man being an asset in a crisis. He put any memories of snakes and toilets firmly from his mind and watched the butler sign up for whatever was required. Next, a rather sheepish Ramsay Sandilands stepped through the door to offer his services while Grimson raised a hand at the back of the room saying "Count me in." Finally, Granville Grimm reminded everyone that Donald Stobo could bring crucial practical skills to the project as well.

And so the hit squad was complete. All they had to do now was transform the old pavilion and create "The Halfway House" in a week.

It's Halfway. Aberfintry's New Café

Wording from promotional flier for
The Halfway House

27. Deadline approaching

"Lachlan Stagg's alive?" squealed Bonnie in disbelief.

"That old rascal," said Grandad with a chuckle. "He always did do things his own way."

Back in Aberfintry, Rory was finding that he had even more explaining to do than after his previous visits. They all agreed that the resurrected local celebrity was an ace up their sleeve in the fight to finally present some facts about Hotel Grimm. However, Bonnie and Gandad moved from surprise to deep apprehension as Rory revealed the launch plans for The Halfway House.

"In seven days!" said Bonnie. "I thought you said the place was a wreck."

"That's ambitious to say the least, son," remarked Grandad.

"Well there is multi-world-record breaker in charge," said Rory trying to convince himself as well as the others, but he could tell that they had concerns that the rest of the team was a motley crew comprising a cable car mechanic, an overweight office executive, a decrepit butler and a reclusive father and son.

Rory said that their job down in Aberfintry was to work on the advertising for The Halfway House and to produce a rival campaign with a grand opening that would deliberately clash with

Saturday's demonstration. Bonnie took notes as Rory and Grandad shouted ideas, but although they began enthusiastically, they couldn't help but dwell on the fact that the campaign for closure was gathering speed. Its advantage wasn't just the fact that the local newspaper was churning out campaign reminders, but the fact that the people who were involved had loud mouths and were having no problem having their message heard. They also had a sympathetic audience in Aberfintry's residents, who had quite simply had enough of Hotel Grimm.

Rory got Grimson to come up with ideas for a flier for the Halfway House and he did an amazing job, producing a stylish, professional and very unusual design. Bonnie suggested putting the fliers under the windscreen wipers of every car in town, enlisting Grimson and Stobo to do the deed. The pair of them leafleted the whole of Aberfintry under cover of darkness one night and the town's residents awoke to find details of an alternative way of spending their forthcoming Saturday morning.

If Rory's campaign had anything in its favour, it was the air of mystery. The flier presented simple facts; a new café would open on Saturday at a mystery location to be revealed on the day; the venue would be announced at 11:15am by a local celebrity who would appear at the demonstration; potential customers could walk to the venue or an unusual kind of lift would be offered to those requiring transport. It certainly got people talking.

"Do you think Zizz Boy is the local celebrity? Surely even he wouldn't stoop to calling himself that?"

"What about Bella Valentine? She likes her cakes. She'd be the perfect person to declare a café open."

"It's a bit strange that we don't know where it's going to be."

"What's the unusual transport do you think? A ferryboat across the River Fintry?"

Grimson's artwork also caused a stir. Mr Boswall, the art teacher, even mentioned it in class. "I want you all to take note of this design. It's simple, yet striking, and whoever did it has real talent. I, for one, am very interested in finding out more about this café and particularly the artist they have commissioned.

Rory scribbled a quick note to let Grimson Grimm know that he might want to consider staging his first ever exhibition at The Halfway House. Sprinting to the cable car station, he dropped the envelope off with Stobo.

"Could you get this up to Grimson, please?" he said handing it over.

"Aye," said the wee man taking the letter without a second glance. Rory was about to go when he thought better of it and turned back.

"How's it going up there?" he asked. "How's the pavilion looking?"

"It's a wreck," said Stobo. Rory's face fell in disappointment. "But come the weekend it'll be fine," he added with a hint of a smile.

Starting to leave, and relieved that Stobo seemed confident in his own abrupt way, Rory stopped as the mechanic called after him.

"Do you think anyone will come?"

"I just don't know what's going to happen," said Rory. "People are talking about it and they're all curious and want to know more. The big question is how will they react when they discover where it is and who's involved?"

Rory tried to blank from his mind the fact that if school was the gauge of local feeling then there wouldn't be any passengers for the cable car on Saturday, just a shouting mob demanding closure.

Halfway through the week, Rory met Grimson at Stobo's workshop. He reported good progress. His father had produced old photos of the pavilion to work from and Lachlan Stagg had used his architectural skills to produce designs. Stagg had also shown that there was still something left of the stamina and determination that had won him six consecutive Scrab Hill Races all those years ago. "He works around the clock," said Grimson, "and he whizzes around the place on a unicycle. You have to see it to believe it!"

Finkleman was also proving that despite his hands going soft in recent years, he still knew exactly what to do, handling tools like he'd been doing it all his life. He had also used some impressive negotiating skills to make sure that the materials they needed were getting to the site, transported up the hill in the cable car. "If I can get shipments of cans to the four corners of the world I can sure get some wood, glass, screws and nails halfway up a hillside," he said as he made his umpteenth phone call of the day.

Meanwhile, Ramsay Sandilands had been hard

at work perfecting recipes, testing them out on the workforce at every tea break, and had also taken responsibility for sorting out the interior design of the new café.

Grog and Stobo were working like pack-horses according to Grimson. "I'm supposed to be the young fit one, but you should see these guys just getting their heads down and getting on with it."

For all the news of progress though, the mood in the town seemed so fervently against the hotel that Rory couldn't help but feel affected. He was beginning to see no way that the campaign for closure could fail. He was coming to the conclusion that it might be a clever idea to have a café in a neutral place that gave people a different view, but it wasn't really clever if no one was going to visit it.

"When people feel so strongly about an issue in these kinds of numbers you're never going to change their minds, are you?" he said in one of his gloomier moments.

"We've got to be positive, Rory," said Bonnie. "What hope is there if the people who believe that something is wrong, decide not to make a noise about it? How will anything ever change?"

Rory knew she had a point, but he just couldn't see how they could make a dent in the strength of opinion that gripped the town.

"I don't disagree with you, Bonnie," said Grandad, "but Rory's right that it's a big challenge. To stand up and keep standing up in the face of all these people takes a strong spirit, a brave heart and a clear voice."

"You're right, Mr Munro," said Bonnie. "Sometimes you have to push yourself even when you don't want to." She nodded to the white stick that Grandad said he hated so much. Grandad scowled at her and mumbled something about everyone being free to choose how much they wanted to do.

To Rory it just felt hard to stand up in a crowd and be a lone voice. Him against them. But then again, he knew that Bonnie was right. With a heavy heart, Rory realized that whatever happened next it was not going to be straightforward. Do nothing and he would brood about it as the mob won the day. Do something and he was effectively setting himself up as a target.

As they spent the end of Friday afternoon together it seemed that there was nothing more that could be done and eventually Grandad gave them their cue to leave.

"I'm puffed out kids," said Grandad. "I'm going to have a doze."

Wish I could do that too, thought Rory. *Easy life just sitting in a chair all day.* He immediately felt bad for thinking it.

Rory and Bonnie left with strict instructions from Grandad to keep him posted about what happened the next morning at the demonstration.

"I'll even check my phone to see if you've texted me," said Grandad.

"Any chance of a reply?" asked Rory.

"Don't push your luck, son. Now all the very best. You can only do what you can do. Right Bonnie?" said Grandad.

"You said it, Mr Munro."

28. The advance party

Saturday dawned bright and clear and Rory woke earlier than usual. Much earlier than usual. His stomach felt like it had tied itself in a complicated knot during the night and, once he was awake, there was no way he was going back to sleep. He knew that he had done everything that was in his power and could only hope that on Scrab Hill the final plans were coming together before the official opening of the café. Part of him couldn't help wondering if it was really worth any last-minute rush since the likelihood was that no one would go up there anyway.

As he dressed he found himself hoping that somehow the population of Aberfintry would wake up open-minded and with a change of heart, but he soon dismissed the idea as fantasy and slumped into a pessimistic mood all over again. He went through the motions of making breakfast but ended up just toying with the cereal in his bowl and nibbling at the edge of a slice of toast.

His Dad joined him in the kitchen as he sat there.

"Got a lesson?" asked Rory.

"Yep. Someone else starting out. Their first lesson," said his Dad. "I can hardly wait to show them the usual routes. Round and round the town at a jerky ten miles an hour." He didn't sounded too cheerful about the prospect but Rory was in no mood to try to brighten up his day. Mr McKenna then opened the morning's paper to read as he crunched his toast loudly, so the conversation was over.

Momo breezed into the kitchen wearing a maroon kimono covered in silver and gold dragons and birds. "Good morning! It's a beautiful day, isn't it!" she breathed. "My, you two make a fine pair. I feel the rain clouds are gathering already with your faces tripping you up!" Rory and his Dad both mumbled their own responses at the same time.

"Rory, I am very excited about The Halfway House," said Momo as she filled the kettle. "I, for one, shall be up there this morning." Rory nodded and tried to block from his mind the thought that this fact might put others off from coming.

His Dad looked up momentarily from the paper. "I've got an eleven o'clock lesson but um … all the best," he said.

The clock seemed to tick around more and more slowly and the knot in Rory's stomach twisted tighter and tighter as the morning went on. Eventually, he couldn't stand kicking around the house any longer, and feeling ill at the prospect, he set off for Lachlan Stagg's statue to see just what kind of response the demonstration had managed to trigger.

He met Bonnie as arranged at the end of Boglehole Road, becoming gradually aware of more and more people walking in the same direction. Rory kept his head down and he and Bonnie remained in silence, both convinced that some of the crowd were throwing hostile glances towards them. Passing number 47, Rory noticed that his Grandad's curtains were still shut. He thought about looking in to the house, but decided to leave it until later when they could report back on how badly things had gone.

As they got further into town the crowd grew in number, and people of every age emerged from each side street he passed. There were boys, girls, men, women, young people, older people and whole families complete with toddlers in pushchairs. Some were carrying placards with slogans like "CLOSE YOUR DOORS FOR GOOD," "GRIMM MUST GO" or "TIME UP" Rory noticed some familiar faces in the crowd; Mrs Trinder-Kerr, Marnie di Angelo with her parents and two brothers and Mr Boswall, the art teacher.

Momo might have thought that "Half Measures" could be a movement, but Rory felt he was walking along as part of a group of people who were all united in one "full" measure. This was without a doubt an exceptional day in the life of Aberfintry and rounding the last corner to the library he saw an enormous gathering around the statue. Malky Mackay stood nearby like a crane, keeping a watchful eye over the growing crowd.

"I think we might just be a teensy weensy bit outnumbered," said Bonnie.

"This is awful. I knew I should have stayed at home today," said Rory. He reached for his phone and texted Grandad. "Bad start. Hundreds here."

The crowd had clustered around a podium on which Derek Goodman was standing, ready to speak into a microphone. Above him the statue of Lachlan Stagg was poised, as ever, for action. Even though Rory knew that the real Stagg would shortly make an appearance, the weight of numbers that had gathered made him fear for the outcome of the morning. As Rory's watch reached 11am, Goodman began to speak.

"Good morning, people of Aberfintry," he said. "And this *is* a good morning as we gather here together for a common purpose." As Goodman continued, it sounded to Rory horribly like so many *Chronicle* articles he had read in recent weeks.

"I think we are all agreed that something must be done," said Goodman. "I call on the hotel to close its doors for good, and for Granville Grimm to leave our community. His establishment has brought pain and shame to us all and we want it no more. Our town should thrive but as long as Scrab Hill is topped by that monstrosity it never will."

Goodman even introduced Bella Valentine to add her voice to the proceedings. She heaved herself on to the podium to declare that it was time to banish everything evil that lurked within the walls of Hotel Grimm. Goodman went on to thank people for signing the petition, highlighting that they had almost gathered every signature in the town. Rory could have sworn that the editor cast a look in his direction as he stated this.

"The next step today is to march to the cable car station," announced Goodman. "I know that some of you rightly fear that place, but let us be assured of the safety and strength in our numbers. We will deliver the petition there and demand that it is taken up to the hotel. From there our campaign will go through every council, court and authority connected with public safety in the country to ensure that they know that the town has spoken and demands action. We will do our utmost to make sure the message is heard and that we see an end to Hotel Grimm. I thank you for your support. Now let us march together."

A cheer went up from the crowd as Bonnie nudged Rory. "Come on. If we're going to do something it has to be now."

Rory wanted to melt away. How could he speak up against this? His mouth went dry and his heart pounded, but he knew it had to be now.

"Hey, there's the Zizz Boy!" Gracie Goodman had spotted him and seemed to sense his discomfort. "Are you the local celebrity? Where's this café then?"

"It's nearly quarter past eleven," another voice shouted.

"Perfect time for a latte."

"Hot chocolate for me."

There were chuckles from some of the onlookers and people began nudging each other to point out that Rory had started pushing his way through the crowd.

"Come on, Rory … spill the beans. Where is it? Does it just sell Zizz?"

"Let him speak."

"Yeah it should be a laugh."

"His family are always making an exhibition of themselves!"

"Hey, Goodman. Let the lad have a say before we go on the march."

As Rory reached the front, Derek Goodman gave him a furious look for distracting the demonstration, but then he seemed to think better of it.

"Ladies and gentlemen," he said into the microphone. "Other people appear to have plans to announce something else today. In the interests of giving everyone a fair hearing *The Chronicle* would like to extend a welcome to the town's one and only Rory McKenna to say a few words."

Goodman stood to one side, gesturing him to step up to the podium, fully expecting public ridicule to be the outcome. Rory glanced at his watch. His arrangement with Lachlan Stagg was that he would arrive at 11:20am. It was now 11:17am. The few steps to the microphone seemed like an enormous task and then his Grandad's words came into his head. "It takes a strong spirit, a brave heart and a clear voice."

He walked on to the podium and turned to look out over a sea of now silent faces. He was reminded of the marketing awards ceremony where he stood looking over a giant room full of people, lapping up applause for something he hadn't done.

Some of the crowd were already turning to each other and whispering. He could see from the intense look in Bonnie's eyes that she was urging him on to speak. Derek Goodman and Bella Valentine were standing to one side talking quietly to each other and gesturing that it was nearly time to begin the march.

Looking beyond the crowd in the distance Rory saw the tufts of white hair of Lachlan Stagg and felt a new surge of optimism. He raised his voice. "Today, marks a new day for Hotel Grimm, and you are all invited. Up on the ledge on Scrab Hill a new café has just opened called The Halfway House. If you go there you will see this town in a whole *new* way. You can get to it by the cable car."

"Get off!"

"You must be joking!"

"Take the microphone off him!"

Rory raised his voice as loud as he could. "To officially open the café today, can I please introduce our mystery celebrity …" Rory pointed over people's heads and with that introduction, Lachlan Stagg reached the back of the crowd. It began to part, people falling backwards and pulling each other out of the way to let him through. There were gasps from many.

"It's him."

"That's impossible."

"It must be him. Look at his ear."

"But he's dead!"

"This town is getting way too creepy for me."

"Hasn't he put on weight since that statue was made?"

Stagg came right to the front and stepped on to the podium as Rory stood to one side. He faced the people of Aberfintry who, after buzzing at his arrival, had fallen silent. Rory looked over and saw that Derek Goodman was ashen-faced as Stagg began to speak.

"My name is Lachlan Stagg and I have some thanks and some apologies to make. Firstly, I would like to thank you, the townspeople of Aberfintry, for continuing to think of me after my … departure, to the extent of building this magnificent statue." He gestured to his rather slimmer twin, cast in bronze above him. "I would never have believed that I was held in this type of regard and I am deeply honoured. Secondly, I would also like to apologize to you. In my efforts to amass my collection of records, I have deceived you all. I did it with the best of intentions. I believed that I could gather the last of my records, including the one for the longest disappearance, and put Hotel Grimm on the map for a good, positive reason, to try to make up for years of difficult times that they had experienced. Ladies and gentlemen, I can tell you that I have been living at Hotel Grimm all these years and I have survived … not because I am exceptional in any way, but because there is *nothing* to fear at Hotel Grimm."

"The place has had more than its fair share of misfortune. In fact, I am sure it could gain its own record for that alone. Latterly, my actions have contributed to their problems, notably *my* attempts to remain hidden led to the suggestion that a beast lived within the hotel walls. There is no beast. Only an eccentric man whose efforts to stay hidden went a little too far."

Rory noticed that in contrast to Derek Goodman's white face, Bella Valentine had gone a shade between bright pink and purple. Stagg continued.

"I am truly sorry. Today, I will go further than just saying that there is nothing to fear on Scrab Hill. I believe that in Hotel Grimm we actually have an example of how to treat one other. For years, Granville Grimm has dealt with the pain of losing his beloved wife, Gwendolen, and of seeing his hotel go virtually out of business. This has presented him with an extremely difficult time. Throughout this period, however, he has not received an ounce of sympathy from this town. Not an ounce! In fact, following a series of unfortunate accidents, none of which had any link to his family, or to any wrong-doing or neglect, he was turned into some kind of monster in people's eyes and made an outcast. How has he responded? He has not reacted angrily. Then, only last week when I revealed my own deception that had, in part, contributed to the downfall of his business, he displayed a wealth of warmth and forgiveness. He is a good and fair man and I commend to you Aberfintry's new café, The Halfway House. It is a remarkable place, it will put the town on the map and it is open....now! Please join me on Aberfintry's very own unique cable car in a journey up Scrab Hill to see it for yourselves."

Rory looked around the faces in the crowd. This had been a mob set on action. Today was the day when they had to stand up and be counted and they were all here. Today was the day that things were to change in their town. As he looked at them, most of them now seemed to be in a state of shock. Some people were quietly lowering the placards they had brought and looking embarrassed about where to put them. Rory saw Malky Mackay with his arms folded giving a slow satisfied nod. He saw Deirdre Dunbar's eyes flitting over to her boss and back again to Lachlan Stagg. He saw Max Fletcher holding what looked like a sack full of the latest edition of *The Chronicle* that he wanted to quietly lose somewhere.

No face had a more confused mix of emotions than Derek Goodman's. His victorious determination of a few minutes before had turned into utter disbelief. Lachlan Stagg who the paper had held up as the town's dead hero and symbol of all that was right, was now alive and proclaiming Hotel Grimm as an example for the town to follow.

Rory looked across at Bonnie in the crowd. She raised her clenched fists and gave a silent victory cheer and then much to Rory's surprise she shouted out to the crowd, puncturing the silence left after Lachlan Stagg's epic speech.

"I'll join you, Mr Stagg. I fancy a hot chocolate and I've always wanted to go in that cable car." Rory grinned at her. Her chair buzzed into life but before she could leave another voice from the back of the crowd shouted.

"Hold on there. Don't go without me!" There was a tapping noise. "I want to see this for myself. Where's Rory?"

The crowd parted as Rory's Grandad worked his way unsteadily through the throng of people. He was leaning on Momo's arm and in his other hand he held his white stick. Unused to using it he was clipping people's ankles with it as the pair pushed their way through. Aware that the large crowd were focusing their attention on him, Rory's Grandad turned to face them.

"What are you all gawping at? Never seen an old boy out and about? Reports of my death have been greatly exaggerated, you know. Good to see you, Lachlan, you mad old rascal."

He reached Rory. "I couldn't work out how to text you a reply so I thought I'd better come down instead. Now can you make sure I don't trip over anything on the way to this cable car? And I would like a window seat in this café too if you can see to it."

"And you lot," he continued, waving his white stick in the air. "Some of you should be ashamed of yourselves. There are people who sadly can't be here today, who would be horrified that this was how things had turned out." Grandad looked meaningfully in Derek Goodman's direction. "It's time that people in this town got a grip on their imaginations and started seeing things properly. Get yourselves up that hill."

With that Grandad hobbled off, heading in the direction of the fast-disappearing Bonnie, dragging Momo with him and barking, "Come on then," at Rory and Lachlan Stagg.

The crowd remained silent and watched them go.

Within minutes the five of them were being ushered into the cable car by Stobo. The normally oily mechanic was wearing a fresh pair of overalls that were so new they still had deep creases in them from where they had been folded in the packaging. Stobo shut the doors with a firm hand. He looked Rory straight in the eye and gave a slight nod as if to note that all was well. Going behind the control desk, he pushed the buttons and Rory saw the glint of a smile on the man's face as he sent them clanking and rocking slowly on their way.

Inside the cable car the group fell silent as they moved out of the housing of the station and began gaining height rapidly. Bonnie was the first to speak. "This is fantastic! WooHoo!"

"What a view!" said Momo. She had already found one of the telescopes and was scanning the landscape below. The car rose and lifted over the first pylon and Aberfintry dropped away below them. "I don't know what Gordon and Gracie were complaining about," said Bonnie with a mischievous look in her eye, craning her neck to see as well as she could out of the window.

"Come on then. Someone describe it to me," said Grandad. The others looked at each other to see who was going to start.

"Don't all shout at once," said Grandad. "Hurry up, I might be missing something important."

"The town is getting so small it looks like a model," said Rory.

"It looks pretty from up here," said Bonnie. "Little streets and matchstick people."

"We can see the park, Dad," said Momo. "It's a splash of colour just like it always was."

"You can see the path where the old Scrab Hill Race used to be," said Lachlan Stagg. "You won that once, Hugh, didn't you?"

"Aye, I did indeed," said Grandad.

"I didn't know that," said Rory turning from the window to look at the old man.

"Oh no, here we go again," said Grandad. "Well it's no secret. The medal is in that box of mine. You need to spend a bit more time in there looking for things."

Rory forced himself to look back at the crowd in the centre of town. They seemed to be milling around but it was impossible to tell what the mood was.

"We're nearly there," said Bonnie. "Hold on, Mr Munro. Stand by for it slowing down."

The station at the ledge came quickly into view, the cable car slowed to half its speed and then came alongside the small building. Grimson was there to greet them. He was dressed in black, as usual, but looking smart and brushed,

"Welcome!" he said. "Would you all like to step this way?" He turned and began to head the short distance down the path to the ledge. As the group followed on, Rory spotted the first thing that had changed since he had been up here last. The new sign read "The Halfway House Café. A warm welcome to all," and just beyond it was something more familiar.

"Grandad. You might remember this," said Rory taking him by the arm and leading him over to the side of the path.

"What is it, son?" said the old man. The wolf statue was standing upright, positioned as the first thing to greet every visitor as they walked from the cable car to the Halfway House.

Grandad dropped his white stick and reached out with both hands, his fingers brushing the stone with tenderness. He whispered to himself as he touched it. It was as though each mark in the stone was one that he remembered making. The group stood back for a moment and watched as he wiped a tear from his eye. Clearing his throat he spoke.

"Know what? Whoever did that had the makings of a master stonemason." His face cracked into a grin. "Come on. What else is there I should see?"

As they walked on, the cable car began its journey back downhill, the little wheels humming on the cables as it went. It seemed as thought Stobo had even found some special grease for the occasion to make things run more smoothly.

"Mmm," said Lachlan Stagg. "If I'm not mistaken that is the smell of a Sandilands Special."

"What's that?" asked Bonnie.

Stagg took a huge sniff of the air. "I think there are fruit scones, ginger snaps, chocolate spice cake and of course a pancake or two."

"Ramsay!" called Rory. A figure in a chef's outfit turned towards him. "Ah, Rory McKenna. Welcome to The Halfway House." Ramsay Sandilands waved grandly around himself. The ledge had been set out with tables, each with a white linen tablecloth, and surrounded by animals — Grandad's stone animals. Stobo had spent some of the week transporting them in a barrow from Grandad's workshop to the cable car. The Curse of the Stonemason had been laid to rest.

In the background the pavilion had been transformed from the shell that Rory had last seen. The glass-walled building stood once more, sitting neatly under the rock overhang. Inside, Rory could see some of Grimson's portraits on display. He could also see Finkleman busying away making tiny adjustments to tables. Even from this distance Rory reckoned that the American had shed a few pounds and benefitted from being out in the sun for a few days. Grog was there too, seated at a cash register near the door. All around the walls was a bank of glass cases; the old fish tanks from the pavilion of years ago. Stepping closer Rory could see that some of Grog's more attractive pets had made the move from the bathroom to a new home at The Halfway House as an additional talking point for guests.

Rory became aware that Bonnie had split from the group and had gone on her own towards the edge of the ledge. He walked over to join her.

"You okay?" asked Rory.

"Yeah," said Bonnie in a quiet voice. "I've never been so high up before. I can see as far as anyone else can. I feel tall, Rory … I actually feel tall!"

Grandad's telescope had been fixed permanently at the edge and Rory looked through the lens, focusing on the scene at the bottom of the hill. What he saw made him stop. Close to the cable car station he could see his father getting out of his car. He removed the learner sign from the roof and tossed it into the boot, before joining the back of a very long queue of people snaking out of the cable station. Rory watched him begin talking to the people he was standing beside, his newspaper uncharacteristically tucked under his arm. Then, emerging from the station, the cable car began its journey up towards the ledge.

"Ramsay!" shouted Rory.

"Yes, my dear boy?"

"Better get ready behind the scenes."

"Why? What is it?" said the whiskery man.

"There's a full cable car on its way and a very long queue for the one after that."

There was a momentary look of disbelief on Ramsay's face but one glance down the hillside confirmed that what Rory had said was true.

"Oh my word, oh my word," said Ramsay bustling about, his nose twitching in anticipation.

"Boys, this is our moment. This is it!" Rory couldn't think at first who Ramsay was talking to and then he twigged.

"Er ... no disrespect, Ramsay, really, but I think you should keep the wee guys out of sight. At least until you get things going." Rory nodded towards a couple of twitching heads in Ramsay's pockets. For a moment Rory thought that he might have touched on Ramsay's raw nerve once again, but the rat collector's face showed a new look of professionalism and determination.

"You're right, Rory McKenna. After all ... you are the marketing genius! You know best!"

"He's right, Rory," said Bonnie looking around at the café. "This is a great piece of work."

"Aye, son," said Grandad. "Not bad for a lad who prefers to sit back a bit!"

A tall figure approached them, coming down the path from the hotel. Granville Grimm's hair was cut short and he wore a dark suit with a bright cravat in the same scarlet colour that Rory remembered from Gwendolen's dress in Grimson's painting.

"Is that who I think it is?" said Bonnie.

"Good morning, Rory," said Granville Grimm as he approached. "How did things go down in the town?".

"Pretty well, I think," replied Rory. "The first customers are on their way."

"Excellent," said Granville Grimm. "I look forward to welcoming them. We've had an amazing week here. I already have so much to thank you for. I think things are finally looking up."

The little group watched as the sun shone on Aberfintry, on Hotel Grimm and on the approaching cable car full of people. They could see the figures inside it pointing to views and to things that they had not seen or not taken the time to look at for years. Granville Grimm was right. Things were definitely looking up for Hotel Grimm.

Later, when Rory thought back on that day, he could picture people stepping falteringly out of the cable car station, not quite sure what they were coming to, only to be met by a fabulous view of their own town and a charming, personal welcome from Granville Grimm. He could see the looks on their faces as they took their first bites of Ramsay's baking and had a clear image of people approaching Grimson and asking him to do portraits for them. By the end of the day he had twelve commissions.

Rory remembered children clustering around the large glass tanks as Grog, dabbing his mouth with a hanky, cheerfully explained for the umpteenth time what all of the creatures were. And beside the till, even Lachlan Stagg's "Beast of Corridor Five" outfit had been displayed — cymbals, bellows, gas-mask and all — but with an additional twist. If you put a coin in a slot in one outstretched hand the dummy clashed, stomped and puffed just like the old days.

Ramsay had even succeeded in keeping his rats out of sight and, to his surprise, Rory even found himself feeling a bit sorry for them. They'd missed out on such a good event.

Meet me up on old Scrab Hill
We'll see what we can see.

Sitting in the Halfway House
We'll have a cup of tea.

Looking down we'll see the town
With pretty little streets,

And count the tiny matchstick folk,
While munching on some treats.

Up above, Grimm Manor,
Towering splendid in the sun

Perfectly crowns the hilltop,
Welcoming everyone.

Winner of The Halfway House competition for their latest advertising campaign (sponsored by The New Aberfintry Chronicle*)*

Epilogue

THE NEW ABERFINTRY

Editorial

Sometime newspaper editors have to take risks. Sometimes they have to go out on a limb, unsure of what the reaction of a readership will be. It is my belief at The Chronicle that Aberfintry is a fine town with equally fine people. That has been made clear in recent days by the willingness of people to be honest and forgiving in a range of remarkable stories. In the past The Chronicle has tried to be an example to the town, but I have seen, in the last few days, that some people in the town have been providing a far better example to this paper and its editor. I have made mistakes and would like to apologise for these. Sometimes personal issues can be so deeply entrenched that they affect how we behave, and that goes on to affect other people. I apologise to Granville Grimm and his family for any hurt caused over the years.

I wish to draw a line and move on. In the spirit of The Halfway House, it is time for a new view and a fresh outlook and thus I hereby launch *The New Aberfintry Chronicle.*

CHRONICLE

FIRST EDITION

Inside this issue:

— Agatha Finkleman and Alistair McGroggan give their recollections of a fiery night at Hotel Grimm and a life-saving act of bravery

— Rats: have we got it all wrong? Scum of the earth, or household pets and companions of the future? Ramsay Sandilands pleads their case.

— Feature: The Curse of the Stonemason: curse or coincidence? We speak to Hugh Munro as he prepares to give his sell-out presentation on stone carving

— Ramsay's Recipes. The master chef from The Halfway House shares some of his tricks of the trade for you to try at home

— Bella Valentine Meets the Beast. We report as Bella Valentine meets the man who was the Beast of Hotel Grimm

— In hiding: Lachlan Stagg talks of his years at the now re-named *Grimm Manor* and his plans for a book on the experience

— Obituary. The Life of Gwendolen Grimm

— Return of the Scrab Hill Race. Entry form on Page 5

— Marketing genius or normal boy? Rory McKenna comes clean about his source of inspiration for the Zizz campaign

Also by Mike Nicholson

In a hidden headquarters below the museum exhibits, there's a gang ready to handle dangerous, spooky or just plain weird problems.

MEET THE

MUSEUM MYSTERY SQUAD

CAN YOU HELP CRACK THE SQUAD'S CRAZY CASES